Blackbeard's Treasure

Blackbeard's Treasure

ILLUSTRATIONS BY
ELISA PAGANELLI

ISZI LAWRENCE

BLOOMSBURY EDUCATION
LONDON OXFORD NEW YORK NEW DELHI SYDNEY

BLOOMSBURY EDUCATION
Bloomsbury Publishing Plc
50 Bedford Square, London, WC1B 3DP, UK
29 Earlsfort Terrace, Dublin 2, Ireland

BLOOMSBURY, BLOOMSBURY EDUCATION and the Diana logo are trademarks
of Bloomsbury Publishing Plc

First published in Great Britain in 2023 by Bloomsbury Publishing Plc.

A catalogue record for this book is available from the British Library

ISBN: PB: 978-1-80199-096-7; ePDF: 978-1-80199-094-3; ePub: 978-1-80199-095-0

2 4 6 8 10 9 7 5 3 1

Typeset by Newgen KnowledgeWorks Pvt. Ltd., Chennai, India
Printed and bound by CPI Group (UK) Ltd, Croydon, CR0 4YY

To find out more about our authors and books visit www.bloomsbury.com
and sign up for our newsletters.

Look out for more books by Iszi Lawrence, published by Bloomsbury.

The Unstoppable Letty Pegg
Billie Swift Takes Flight

Visit www.bloomsbury.com for more information.

For Amy

'Nobody but meself and the Devil knows where it be.
And the longest liver should take all.'

Edward Thatch, 1718

CHAPTER ONE

The Pirate Attack on Sandy Point

1st December 1717

'Marry me and I'll take you to Madagascar and we will set up a pirate kingdom and slaughter the British dogs!' The boy said, triumphantly waving a stick over his head.

Abigail sat under her parasol, amidst the various rocks, sticks and flowers that represented her treasure. She raised an eyebrow. 'It wouldn't have happened like that.'

'It did!' he said. 'The pirates overcame the Mughal warriors and won the heart of the princess.'

'But why would a sultan's daughter agree to marry Captain Avery, when he just killed her friends and took her ship?' She gestured at the broken lopsided cart that was representing the mighty flagship.

'It wasn't *her* ship. Girls don't own ships.'

'If it was a boy's ship then how come it was full of jewels?' Abigail got up in a huff, dropping the orange which was supposed to be her royal orb and knocking over her parasol sceptre.

'Me booty!' The boy pretended to fall over in despair as the fruit rolled gently down the hill towards the great house.

'Shhh!' Abigail said but it was too late.

Nanny Inna came out of the house and marched up the hill towards them. It wasn't until she was a few yards away that they could hear what she was shouting.

'Achu! Boubacar, you depraved child, leave Master Buckler's daughter alone.'

'We weren't doing anything, Mama,' he said, dropping the stick and quickly removing the kerchief from his head.

'Two days after harvest and already you're running around like a rabid dog, when your brothers are still sick from work.' She began shouting at him in her native language, speaking too quickly for Abigail to understand.

'Mi nanataa Fulfulde! So speak English!' Abigail said.

'Have you been teaching her Fulfulde?!' Nanna Inna looked horrified.

'She's really good,' Boubacar nodded.

'I taught Boubacar some Dutch, too,' Abigail said happily but Nanny Inna wasn't pleased.

'Master Buckler is going to be livid if he finds out his child speaks like us. You terrible boy! I should spank you right here!'

'Leave him alone,' Abigail ordered. She deepened her voice to sound like her father.

'Miss Buckler, Boubacar may have lighter skin that me but he is still a slave and he will get himself killed if he's not careful.' Nanny Inna's voice changed from soothing to near screaming as she barged past Abigail and threw a pebble at her son. Boubacar cowered behind the cart. 'If a nasara sees you with a master's child, a daughter no less, they'll punish us all along with you! Alla hiin'en e sarriiji Seyðaani…'

A wild velvet monkey scurried down from the tree at the back of the garden. The monkeys had been brought over by the French who used to rule the island. They were pets but had escaped to the mountains and multiplied. They caused nothing but mischief. The monkey sidled up to the orange on the garden path. Abigail started after it.

'Stop! Arrête!'

It grabbed the orange with both paws and darted back, jumping into a tree and then down into the rows of young sugarcane on the other side of the garden wall.

When she turned back, Nanny Inna had Boubacar by the arm and was dragging him to the kitchen door. Abigail sighed and then, still under the shade of her parasol, walked leisurely back to the house. The cool darkness enveloped her.

The house was not its usual tidy calm. There were men's satchels in the hallway and dusty coats draped over the surfaces. Her father had been up for the past two nights, along with nearly everyone at Sandy Point. The sugarcane harvest had to be processed immediately or it would sour so slaves worked without sleep, and free men snatched a few hours when they could.

Abigail crept quietly to the door of her father's office. Inside, the voices of men rumbled and erupted in coughing and laughter. Suddenly, one of her father's friends, Mr Oultram, rounded the corner, coming from the front door. He was sweating, and covered in dust from the path up to the house.

'How do you do?' he said curtly. 'Is your father home?'

Of course he was home. Mr Oultram had just caught her eavesdropping on him. She shrugged and turned away.

'Young lady,' he called after her. 'The Africans in the fields have better manners than you, and they haven't had a fraction of your advantages.'

Abigail's cheeks reddened. She didn't like being told off. 'My father owns this plantation. You can't tell me what to do. You're just a merchant.'

Mr Oultram shook his head. 'You don't champion your father by besmirching my profession. Good day, Miss Buckler.'

She tried to think of something very rude to say to Mr Oultram but he'd already gone into her father's office.

The office overlooked the front of the house, past the sugarcane fields and down towards the town of Sandy Point. When the office door swung open, Abigail briefly heard the faint chime of the warning bell coming through the open window before the door shut in her face. She stood alone in the corridor trying to hear what the men were saying. Moments later, Abigail's father and the rest of the men barged out through the door. Some were still holding their cups. They ignored her and marched out towards the entrance. The warning bell grew loud again as the front door opened and the men stampeded down the hill. Her father didn't follow them. He stood in the entrance hall, shouting for Nanny Inna to bring him his uniform. To Abigail's shock, he was taking off his clothes, scattering them all over the floor. Nanny Inna quickly appeared with a bundle of clothing. As he tried to get his belly into his britches Abigail seized this rare opportunity to talk with him.

'I've learnt some Portuguese,' she said confidently. 'Você está feliz comigo, pai?'

'Not now,' he muttered, trying to do up his waistcoat.

'Aren't you going to be hot?' Abigail asked. Her father's face turned the same colour as his coat.

'Go and wait in the kitchen, child,' Nanny Inna said sweetly as she picked up his dirty breeches.

'No, her and the boy are coming with me.'

'To battle?' Boubacar asked, looking up from polishing his master's boot.

Nanny Inna shushed him.

'To the fort. Safest place.'

'But Papa, the French won't destroy the house…' Abigail began.

'It's not the French,' he snapped at her. 'It's pirates.'

'Why can't we stay here?'

'This isn't just a ragtag ship. It's an entire fleet about to raid every boat at Sandy Point.' Major Buckler shook his head. 'Pirates have been known to lay waste to entire towns.'

'Will they take the harvest?' Abigail gasped.

'I imagine that is exactly what they plan to do,' Major Buckler snapped. 'Here, carry the flasks.'

'Why does *he* have to come?' Abigail asked, watching Boubacar slip the loops of leather over his head so that the flasks dangled around him like an enormous necklace.

She felt resentful that Boubacar, despite being a slave, got all her father's attention. He was training him to be a clerk while Abigail had French lessons from a governess at the Phipps' estate and rarely saw her father at all.

'The boy will be safer in the fort. If they get him,' Major Buckler indicated at Boubacar, 'they'll keep him. Either to turn pirate or to sell. Skilled slaves fetch a lot more.'

'Fine by me,' Boubacar whispered to Abigail. She nearly laughed.

'What about Nanny Inna?' Abigail said.

'I'll go up to the village and warn anyone there to stay away from the docks,' Nanny Inna said. 'We will hide in the forest if any pirates come to kidnap us.'

'Would they kidnap me, Father? Would I be made a slave?' Abigail asked as he checked his rifle. 'Would I cost more than Boubacar?'

'Don't wish that on yourself for a second, child,' Nanny Inna admonished her.

'You're a girl. An ugly one at that. You'd barely fetch more than my boots,' Boubacar said, winking.

Abigail's cheeks flushed. Nanny Inna looked nervously at her master but he was too distracted with his buckles to notice.

'Onward!' Major Buckler said.

Both children turned to wave back to Nanny Inna, before following him out of the house.

It was a short walk down the hill. Abigail could see masts peaking over the tops of the shacks and houses on the haphazard waterfront. She couldn't stop to take a look. Abigail's father steered them away from the seafront.

Militiamen were running the opposite direction along the road.

'Charles Fort!' bellowed Major Buckler, stopping to wave at them. 'Not Fort Charles! You're going the wrong way!'

The group stopped and waved back. They then proceeded to split in two, run in opposite directions and, realising the others weren't following, double back on themselves and collide in the middle.

'I bet it was that jackanapes Phipps, telling the men the wrong fort. You know that man brands his slaves?'

'That's terrible,' Abigail said. She'd once burnt her hand on the kettle and it hurt for days, and that wasn't hot enough to leave a scar. She couldn't imagine how painful it would be to be branded; suddenly the idea of being captured by the pirates became a lot more scary.

'It is terrible!' her father continued, but he wasn't thinking about how it must hurt. 'Branding devalues slaves completely. What if he ever has to sell them?'

Boubacar was struggling to stay quiet. Abigail could tell he was angry that her father didn't care about the suffering that branding caused.

'If the pirates catch us, they won't brand us, will they?' Abigail asked quickly. She didn't want Boubacar to get into trouble. If he spoke back to her father, he would be punished for it.

'They aren't going to capture either of you, I'll see to that,' Major Buckler said confidently, dropping his pouch of gunpowder.

Boubacar picked it up and handed it to him, sharing a disbelieving look with Abigail.

She giggled, moving her parasol so that her father wouldn't catch her.

There was musket fire in the distance and then the boom of a cannon.

'Are we going to Charles Fort?' Abigail asked nervously.

'No, we're going up to the fort at Brimstone Hill.'

'Shouldn't we be helping to fight?' Boubacar asked.

Major Buckler took this badly, as though Boubacar had accused him of being cowardly. 'Brimstone Hill looks over the entire bay! Fighting isn't just combat.'

'Isn't it?'

'No! Someone needs to oversee everything. There are still a couple of working cannons up there. We can help protect Fort Charles… I mean Charles Fort!'

They headed up the hill to the unfinished fortress on the mountainside, the path was littered with the long sugarcane leaves. They looked like cutlass blades. Abigail jumped as she heard the boom of a cannon.

'If it comes to it, we can hide in the forest,' Boubacar said.

Abigail agreed. 'Meet me by the saman tree on the path behind the house.'

He nodded and they marched on. Abigail's dress clung to her back with sweat. When they were halfway up, they were joined by more men in red coats slowing down to speak to her father.

'Sir, we're worried what the slaves will do if the pirates make land,' he panted. 'Should we punish one publicly now, to remind the others to keep in line?'

Abigail moved her parasol in front of Boubacar to hide him from the red coat's eye.

'Not in front of the children, gentlemen,' her father replied. He turned to Abigail and Boubacar. 'Hurry up you two.'

Once they reached the fort, Boubacar and Abigail rested next to a pile of cut square cobbles. The building works were thick with weeds.

'Major Buckler!' It was one of Abigail's father's friends, whose red coat barely fitted over his round stomach.

'Is it true there is more than one ship?' wheezed Abigail's father, still out of breath from climbing the hill.

'Two sloops and a galleon.'

'Why have the cannon stopped firing?'

'Sir, it was *L'Océan* that was firing. They've boarded her and the other merchant vessels in the anchorage.'

'Charles Fort hasn't been defending her?'

'Saving the powder.'

'That's my harvest! Signal to Charles Fort right now to fire those cannon!'

It was at this point in the conversation that Abigail backed away and followed Boubacar up the steps to the top of the fortress wall.

The wind was strong and she dropped her parasol. The King's colours were flying above. The rope slapped against the flagpole in the sea breeze.

Looking down into the harbour, Abigail could see that one of the pirate sloops was broadside with

L'Océan. The pirates were hurriedly transferring hogsheads of sugar and barrels of rum into a jolly boat. The sails of the pirate sloop were slacked off and the wind billowed through them. It gave Abigail the impression they were greedily snatching at the merchant ship like a velvet monkey after fruit. She wanted to see the faces of the pirates themselves, but they were too far away.

'Here, have a look!' Boubacar handed her a telescope.

'What is that?!'

'It's called a glass. The surgeon comes up here at night to look at the stars.' He pointed over to a collection of objects propped against the wall. A chair, a blanket, and a collection of poles like a sheerlegs or easel.

'You pinched it?!'

'I'll put it back when we're done,' Boubacar said.

The leather tube was heavier than Abigail had imagined and so she rested her elbow on the fortress wall and peaked through. At first she saw nothing, just black and then a flash of blue.

She followed the little patch of colour until it popped into focus. She gasped. The flat sea in the bay was wrinkled with waves. She could see the grinning faces of the pirates and the flash of oars in the sinking sun.

Abigail's eye travelled at once to the majestic flagship.

'Their flag is a skeleton and cutlass.'

'Let me see!' Boubacar took back the telescope. 'She's room for forty cannon. She must be super fast with a keel that long! How did pirates manage to capture her?'

They must really be in league with the Devil, Abigail thought.

'What are they doing to *L'Océan*?' Abigail watched as the merchant ship's sails were unfurled and set.

'They couldn't have unloaded her,' Boubacar said. 'It took all day to load her up.'

'Maybe they are going to commandeer her...'

But there weren't enough men left onboard. *L'Océan* drifted haphazardly, not out to sea, but towards the shore and Charles Fort. She came to an abrupt halt, presumably stuck on a reef.

The cannon beneath them finally boomed. Both the children clutched their ears as dust rose around them. The aim was off. The rounds hit the shoreline, upsetting sea birds. The children watched horrified as the pirates set light to *L'Océan*. The cannon ports on the ship began to glow orange. The cannon at Charles Fort boomed again. Another miss.

The poor ship crackled as the flames rose higher, consuming the masts, sails and cargo. All that sugar that the plantation had worked so hard to get was gone.

'What was the point in that?' Boubacar yelled. 'You idiots! Why? Are they stupid?'

The acrid smell of the burning timber and sugar blew in from the sea. It made Abigail retch. She took back the telescope and focused again on the flagship. She was broadside to Charles Fort, ready at any moment to fire her cannon. Abigail could just make out her name through the rising smoke. *Queen Anne's Revenge.*

It was obvious to Abigail who the captain was. He stood perfectly still on the quarterdeck, while colourfully dressed pirates swarmed around him. He was lean, dressed finely in a dark frock coat and had an enormous black beard, which was twisted into braids. The moment she focused the telescope on him, he turned his head and stared straight back at her. It was as though he could see into her mind.

She let out an involuntary squeak and dropped the telescope.

The Charles Fort cannon fired again and, this time, *Queen Anne's Revenge* responded. All her cannon boomed as one, rocking the ship. Charles Fort was smashed with a direct hit to its seawall. Men were buried under rubble, *L'Océan* was splintered by shrapnel, sending sparks into the evening sky. Abigail lifted the telescope to her eye once more and watched as men tried to get back to their battered guns but it was already too late. The pirates were heading out of the harbour. Every vessel left in the anchorage was on fire.

CHAPTER TWO
Captain Charles Vane

18 April 1718

Abigail sat watching the twins hit each other. Mrs Phipps continued to sew. The Phipps' slaves tended the garden in the heat. The white women and children stayed cool in the shade of three large parasols.

'Doe voorzichtig! Take care. This is something that will pass down the generations,' Mrs Phipps said.

Not in my family, thought Abigail, unpicking a stitch. In a fair world, Abigail would be making a quilt with her mother, who would still be alive.

'Doe voorzichtig,' Mrs Phipps said again, pointing at Abigail's uneven stitches.

Do-four-s-ich-t-ich. She loved the crunchy sound of Dutch words. It required you to make the noise of the sea sweeping up the beach in the back of your throat. The Dutch language was the only good thing about being in Mrs Phipps's company. When Abigail's mother had died, the Phipps family had offered to look after her. Abigail's father had gleefully welcomed having his daughter out from under his feet and helped pay for their governess, a Spanish girl who taught Abigail French.

Abigail was getting better at understanding both Dutch and Spanish, although she kept this to herself. She didn't want anyone to know she could overhear their secrets.

''ow you say, I meelked de cow for to make some cheese?' asked Isabella, her tutor.

'J'ai trait la vache et fait du fromage.'

'You need to connect dees ideas. So, I meelked the cow pour faire du fromage. Para comer. Entiendes?'

'Er, the children have…'

'En français, s'il vous plait, mademoiselle.'

'Les enfants jouent au soleil.'

Isabella saw the toddlers had moved into the sun. '¡Señora Phipps! Los niños se quemarán al sol…'

'Breng ze door, ik ben er zo.' Mrs Phipps gathered the children and handed Abigail the patch she was working on. 'Continue. We won't be long.'

Once Abigail was sure both women were back in the house, she dumped the patchwork at her feet and made for the garden wall. A group of slaves were chatting on the other side in an African language. She was disappointed. It was different from the one Boubacar and Nanny Inna spoke. She was missing Boubacar, and wanted to make new friends.

After the pirate attack, her father had been forced to sell slaves to make up for the lost harvest. One of them was Boubacar's older brother, Haruna. Ever since then, Boubacar had not spoken to Abigail, or even glanced at her.

She was furious with him. Boubacar was punishing her for what had happened. It wasn't her fault the harvest was destroyed. It wasn't her fault the banks needed the money. It wasn't her fault her father had sold the slaves. She felt he was being selfish. Now she had no one to play with.

Nanny Inna had always acted like Abigail was a barrel of gunpowder that could explode any second. Boubacar was the only one she could ever really talk to. Now she was alone.

Abigail climbed up the palm and braced herself against the wall, enjoying the chatter of the people, imagining what they might be saying and repeating their words under her breath.

***

'You're like a parrot,' Mr Oultram said to her that evening. 'You sound just like an African merchant I know.'

22

Abigail sat back quietly at the dinner table while her father and Mr Oultram's conversation returned to the attack on Sandy Point last year.

'According to Tibby,' Mr Oultram confided, 'we were attacked as revenge.'

'Revenge for what?'

'For the hanging of the survivors of the pirate ship that sank.'

'The *Whydah*?'

Mr Oultram nodded. 'Thatch, this 'Blackbeard' character...'

'Blackbeard?! What sort of idiotic name is that?'

Abigail immediately thought of the man she had seen on the quarterdeck of *Queen Anne's Revenge*.

'He didn't like us flying the King's colours. Saw it as our tacit agreement with the hangings in Boston.'

'Of course we agree with the hangings!' Major Buckler slammed his fist on the table. 'Black Sam Bellamy robbed and murdered everyone who crossed his path!'

'If he murdered everyone, how do we know his name?' Abigail asked but she was ignored.

'Word is that Cotton Mather heard their confessions and said the pirates had been pressed...' continued Mr Oultram.

'Nonsense! No one is forced into piracy. If they give you a choice to be a pirate or die, you save your soul and you die,' Major Buckler said. 'Pirates have one motivation. Greed.'

Mr Oultram shook his head. 'A lot of them are Jacobites.'

'Codswallop. They think that by claiming King George isn't the real king they can escape punishment. Even if James were king, he'd still have them hanged.'

'It isn't just Blackbeard. There is his friend Hornigold and others. We'd need a fleet to stop them.' Mr Oultram sipped his wine. 'They must be making an absolute fortune.'

'Blackbeard destroyed hundreds of pounds worth of my sugar and rum. How rich do you have to be to burn all that money? And where is he now?'

'He could be anywhere.'

'He's ruined me.' Abigail noticed her father's hands shaking. 'If the next harvest doesn't come through…'

'You can always sell more slaves,' Mr Oultram said wearily.

'No!' Abigail blurted.

Both the men had forgotten she was at the table.

'Bed for you, young lady,' her father said sternly. 'This talk isn't for children.'

Abigail walked up the stairs and into the nursery. She hated seeing her father worried. He shouted a lot more. He drank a lot more. She didn't know how to make it better.

She lay awake, listening to the ocean. It roared like a monster. Somewhere out in its incomprehensible vastness was Blackbeard. He was gloating. No one was going to hold him to account. No one could stop him. Abigail was full of rage. The injustice of it. She angrily turned over and stared blankly at the ceiling.

***

The next morning, Abigail woke to see Nanny Inna chasing an escaped mule down the hill. Abigail's father had passed out in his office. She tidied his papers away so he didn't have to face them when he came round.

Bored, she went for a walk and found two women pulling up weeds at the edge of the newly planted sugarcane crop. They were talking about a galleon that had arrived at Sandy Point that morning. At least, she thought that's what they said. They spoke the same language as Boubacar but faster.

The last galleon Abigail had seen was *Queen Anne's Revenge*. Was Blackbeard back? Would he attack again?

Casting aside her parasol, she dashed between the rows of sugarcane towards the docks. The wind picked up, and the grass whipped around her, waving her on. She came to the end of the field and, grabbing her skirt in her hand, she jumped the ditch.

She ran through another field, the slaves moving out of her way as she stormed past. She punched through a row of older cane and barged into an overseer. He dropped his gun to quickly grab his dog's leash. The salivating jaws were inches from Abigail's leg. She could still hear it barking as she continued to run, her feet patting the mud like Nanny Inna slapping bread dough.

She got to the road. From here she could see the masts in the harbour. She scanned them, but there were no three-mast square rigs in the dock. If *Queen Anne's Revenge* had been here, she had already gone.

Instead of turning back, Abigail thought she'd make sure. The darkening cloudy sky and strong sea breeze lessened the stink of the small town. She ran diagonally across the slave market. It was only busy on Sundays when it was crowded with slaves from the surrounding plantations selling what little they had to each other.

In the anchorage, near the charred remains of *L'Océan*, was a large sloop. She was low in the water, full of cargo. She had obviously been in a battle. There were shrapnel marks all over her hull. Going by the lick of fresh paint on the stern, she had recently been renamed *Ranger*. A torn St George's flag flew from her rigging.

'Gail!'

She knew that voice. Boubacar was leaning against a water butt in the shadow of a building. He was clutching his stomach. He had something running down the side of his head. It was blood.

She ran over. 'What happened?'

'I was crab fishing,' he said. 'Two white fellas took my catch.'

'What did you say to them?'

'What could I say?' he spluttered. 'I told them the catch belonged to my master.'

'And they still took it?'

He jutted his jaw out. 'They beat me first.'

She felt vindicated somehow, that the universe was punishing him for ignoring her. Then she felt bad. He was close to tears. She wanted to hug him to make him feel better but someone might see them and tell her father.

'Did you recognise them?'

He shook his head and she winced as blood oozed out of the small cut in his hairline.

'Did you see where they went?'

'Yeah,' he pointed at the post house.

'Can you stand?'

'Why?' He got up. 'What are you going to do?'

'We are going to get some money to pay for the damage they have done to my father's property.'

'That's a stupid idea.'

'No it isn't. You might get a fever from the cut, plus the rips in your shirt, and the laundry…'

'And the crabs…'

'Never mind the crabs,' she said, 'they can't go around beating people up.'

They walked into Miller's shop which acted as part post house, part apothecary. Half a dead pig hung next to bags of post. Mrs Miller stood in front of shelves of jars, dealing with a well-dressed customer in a Portuguese hat. Her clerk was sorting a great sack of letters. She'd dressed him in a clean white shirt and neat waistcoat. Abigail felt embarrassed by the state of her own slave and dusted Boubacar's shirt sleeve.

Two men were waiting in line at the counter. One was a younger white man wearing colourful calico clothing. The other was light skinned, like Boubacar. The crab bucket was at their feet.

'Excuse me.' Abigail walked straight up to them.

Boubacar grimaced.

'Those crabs belong to my father.'

The colourfully dressed man raised his eyebrows. 'Is that right?'

'Yes,' she said, pointing at Boubacar. 'You've damaged his property and stolen his catch.'

'The boy wouldn't give them over.' The other man shrugged. 'We didn't know who he belonged to. He looked shifty. Needed a slap.'

Abigail puffed herself up. 'That isn't how gentlemen behave!'

'We ain't gentlemen,' he said. 'Go away or it won't just be the boy who gets a beating.'

'Now listen,' she began, oblivious to the danger she was in.

Boubacar, however, could sense it immediately. He stepped forward to stand in front of Abigail. With raised hands he took the blow and fell sideways. The colourfully dressed man stepped forward to grab him, knocking the bucket over.

Crabs and seawater sloshed over the floor.

'Not in my holding!' Mrs Miller pointed at the door. 'You can't come in here and act like Frenchmen.'

Her customer turned round, his hand on the hilt of a cutlass. 'Eddy, Jack. Hop it!'

The two men made their escape, leaving Boubacar to pick up the crabs.

'You're English!' Abigail said, recognising his London accent.

He touched his hat. 'Captain Charles Vane, how do you do?'

'How do you do?' She bobbed a curtsy. 'Miss Abigail Buckler.'

'Buckler?' he repeated. 'I don't come across that name often.'

'I do,' she said meekly, wishing Boubacar would hurry up with the crabs.

Captain Vane smiled. 'You said your father owns a plantation?'

She nodded.

'Which one, my love?'

Abigail's confidence wavered. She felt a chill come over her as the stranger's cool blue eyes met hers.

'Don't you know?' he prompted.

Abigail ignored Boubacar's slow head shake and answered the stranger's question.

'Oh I see. And is your father home?'

Just then, two militiamen, one of whom was Mr Oultram, came into the building.

'Everything in order, Mrs Miller?' Mr Oultram said, surveying the scene: the wet floor, Boubacar's cut, the stranger, and Abigail Buckler, without a parasol, looking worried. 'What's happened?'

'Nothing for you gentlemen to concern yourselves with,' Vane said.

Mr Oultram looked at Abigail's face again, Boubacar's worried expression and back up to Vane. 'Who are you?'

'Captain Vane of *Ranger*.' He removed his hat and bowed.

The second militiaman drew his sword. 'There is a pirate named Vane! Commands a sloop called *Lark*.'

Mr Oultram jumped straight forward, his hand reaching for Captain Vane's hilt to stop him drawing his weapon. Inches from Captain Vane's nose, he looked him right in his eye. 'You deny it?'

'No, but I have a certificate of protection from Alexander Pearse proving I ain't a pirate no more. My crew and I took the King's pardon. I have proof on my ship.'

Mr Oultram didn't back away. 'So you're what now? A merchant?'

'A privateer, I hunt pirates. Word is Blackbeard is coming back to this island.'

Mr Oultram looked over at Boubacar and Abigail. 'You two get back to your father! What are you doing talking to strangers anyway?'

Abigail and Boubacar didn't need telling twice. They ran out into the street.

CHAPTER THREE

The Unexpected Dinner Guest

18 April 1718

'I told you it was a bad idea,' Boubacar said in frustration as they began walking up the hill towards the plantation. It started to rain.

'I did it for you!' Abigail said.

'For me?' he scoffed. 'So I could get hit again? Thank you.'

Abigail didn't like his sarcasm. 'In case we needed money for a doctor. You should be grateful.'

'You don't do anything for me.'

'We don't do anything for you?' She said. 'Who paid for your clothes?'

'I did. My mother did. With the work we do for no money. I have to fetch us crabs for our dinner and sell pots at the market because your father doesn't feed us enough for a rat to live on.'

Abigail blinked in shock. She'd never heard anyone criticise the way her father did things.

'Grain prices...' she began, watching him struggle with the bucket, the cut on his forehead looked redder in the rain.

'He gave us pig feet. He knows we don't eat pork. He's cruel. Nanny Inna says slaves in Africa eat with their masters. Here, mules get more than we do...'

'Well, they work harder!' she snapped back. A pang of guilt washed over her. 'Give me the bucket.'

'No,' he said.

'You're injured. I'll carry it,' she insisted, trying to snatch it away from him.

'I said no.'

She grabbed the bucket handle. 'You have to do what I want!'

'Get off,' Boubacar snarled. 'You're not even allowed to talk to me. And when you tell your darling daddy about this encounter, guess who will end up being flogged for it? It won't be his perfect precious daughter, will it?'

He turned on his heel and walked into a row of sugarcane.

'You can't speak to me like that!' she yelled after him, following him into the field.

The ground became muddy as the skies opened and the rain fell steadily, soaking them both in seconds. She caught up with him, caught his arm and turned him to face her.

'I said you can't speak to me like that!'

'Why not? I'm already going to get whipped for this. How much worse can it get?'

'My father has never whipped you!'

'He locked me in a cupboard for letting a pot boil over!' he yelled back. 'A stupid pot!'

'He would never whip you. He likes you.'

She had nearly said, 'he likes you more than me', but she caught herself in time.

'I hate him,' Boubacar said, turning again into another row of sugarcane, trying to get away from her.

'Slaves, be subject to your masters with all reverence,' she quoted. 'It is in the Bible. How can you hate him? He's kind.'

He stopped and turned around. 'If you think that, you're a fool.'

Abigail started to cry. 'I'm not a fool.'

'Yes you are,' he almost laughed. 'You think you are so much better than me, but one day he'll sell you too. To the richest bridegroom. A wedding band might be more comfortable than chains, but don't pretend you're any less at his mercy than I am.'

'He'll find me a husband who loves me.'

Boubacar rolled his eyes. 'Unless there is money to be made. Think about it, Gail. He doesn't care about anything. Not me, not you, just himself and how he looks to other boring old men.'

'You're wrong!' she shouted back.

Abigail never hated anyone more in her life. They marched in silence back to the house.

***

Abigail didn't tell her father about that afternoon's encounter. She didn't want to worry him with the news that a pirate hunter thought Blackbeard was coming back. She sat with him at dinner, watching him read a ledger.

'Eat your food. It costs enough,' he grunted, not looking up.

She looked down at the grey beef stew Nanny Inna had prepared. Nanny Inna would now be up in the slave village, preparing Boubacar's crabs for her family. Even they had to be nicer than this. Abigail's father seemed to enjoy food most when it was entirely devoid of flavour. 'Anything is a feast when you've been lost at sea,' he would say.

'Master, there is a visitor,' Boubacar appeared at the door, speaking into the room without looking at Major Buckler or Abigail.

'Who?'

'He says his name is Cook,' Boubacar said.

'Cook?' Major Buckler sniffed, plopping his spoon back in the stew. 'What does he look like?'

'English, expensive clothes…'

'Old or young?'

Boubacar thought for a moment. 'Younger than you.'

'Cook…' Major Buckler mused, scratching his ear. 'You'd better show him in.'

Boubacar stayed in the doorway.

'Hurry up, boy.'

'Sir, his name isn't really Cook.' Boubacar looked Major Buckler in the eye. 'He's not an honest man. I think you should hide.'

Abigail gasped.

'What do you mean his name isn't Cook?' said Major Buckler.

'He gave me a false name to tell you.'

'You're accusing him of lying?'

'Yes,' Boubacar said.

Major Buckler narrowed his eyes. 'I suppose your African blood means you think you can tell when someone is lying.'

Boubacar looked confused. 'No master, I am worried for your safety... he told me to tell you he is alone but it isn't true.'

'Enough!' Major Buckler hit the table making the crockery shake. 'You dare accuse a British subject of lying because you can't see past your own dishonest nature?'

Boubacar knew better than to speak.

'Is it Captain Vane?' Abigail asked Boubacar.

The boy looked at Abigail and nodded, his eyes wide.

Major Buckler looked from one to the other, furious. 'Have you been consorting with my daughter?!'

Just before Abigail thought her father would throw his knife at Boubacar, Captain Vane walked in.

'Good evening, Archie.'

'Sir, do I know you?'

'We go way back.' Vane's eyes latched onto Major Buckler like a cat watching a hummingbird.

Abigail slid out from her seat at the table and crept slowly back towards the wall. The heavy dining room door swung open again and two more men strode in. It was the two men from the post house. They had already drawn their cutlasses. Abigail backed away and stood against the far wall, opposite Boubacar. He had stopped the large door from shutting with his foot.

'What brings you to Sandy Point?' Major Buckler tried to sound unintimidated. But his eyes kept jumping to the weapons.

'Privateers,' Vane said. 'We heard Blackbeard was going to pay St Christopher's Island another visit. We was planning to ambush him.'

'They're offering £100 for the head of a pirate captain,' Jack, the man in the colourful calico clothes explained. 'And any pirate who ain't taken the King's pardon is worth £30.'

'We sell captured pirates to you,' Eddy, the other man from the post house, said. 'You claim credit and get the full reward. We get a cut without troubling with the paperwork.'

'Fine.' Major Buckler looked relieved. 'You've come to hear my account of the attack in December?'

'Afraid not, Archie.' Vane smiled. 'This is a personal visit.'

Boubacar signalled to Abigail to come to him. Abigail remained where she was, still too scared to move.

'If you sit, I can get you some food or...'

'You really don't remember me, do you?' Vane said. 'On *Elizabeth*? You were quartermaster when we fought the Spanish.'

'I don't remember.' Major Buckler stood up as Vane advanced.

'Quite the stickler for the rules, you was,' Vane continued. 'When I was sick with fever, you got me scrubbing the orlop, and when I puked all over what I had just polished, you trod on me fingers.'

'You must have me confused with someone else.'

'I thought I might've. But Buckler is an unusual name.'

Boubacar was signalling more urgently for Abigail to cross the room and come to the doorway.

'And seeing your face now,' Vane said sweetly, 'even in the candlelight enjoying your sumptuous dinner, I cast my eye on a visage I recall very well.'

Vane's men chuckled as they moved closer to Major Buckler. Abigail seized her moment and crossed the room. Boubacar, holding the door open with his foot, tried to pull her out but Abigail was too focussed on what the men were saying.

'The last I saw of you,' Vane put his boot on an empty chair, 'was when you ditched me and the boys at Port Royal.'

'The war was over. It was the King's orders,' Major Buckler replied hotly.

'That German oaf ain't our king,' Calico Jack sneered.

'But you're privateers! You work for the King!'

'We lied,' Vane shrugged. 'Just like when you said you would pay us our wages. And you stole them.'

Major Buckler's expression changed from angry confusion to fear.

'Oh, you remember that?' Vane's smile had flipped into a sneer and he got closer to Major Buckler's face. 'You've no recollection of beating McLaren, or keel hauling Jessop, but you remember lining your pockets and waving goodbye when you stranded us in Jamaica. We had no job, no money and no passage back home. I assumed you'd sailed back to England but here you are, a landowner no less.'

'Whatever wrong you feel I have done you, I assure you I was merely obeying my captain.'

'Following orders was you? Is that what you were doing when you hung Billy upside down from the yardarm and lashed him?'

'If you knew anything about running a ship, you'd know the importance of discipline.'

'I do run my own ship. My crew vote on who gets in, who gets a cut and who gets punished.'

'But that's... that's how pirates run their ships!'

Abigail felt Boubacar pulling on her sleeve. As she turned towards him, she missed her father being struck. She heard the sound of a sword whooshing through the air and his chair being knocked backwards.

'Dang it! I wanted the gundiguts alive!' Charles Vane shouted.

She didn't look back. Boubacar pulled her through the door. His grip doubled as he hauled her into the dark entrance hall.

They heard Vane's voice ask, 'Where is the girl?' as they tumbled out of the front door onto the porch.

There were more men waiting by the front gate. Abigail couldn't see their faces, only their torches and swords flashing orange from the flames. She was about to call for help but Boubacar pulled her sideways, behind the bushes at the front of the house.

'They're *his* men,' he whispered, signalling for her to stay quiet.

Abigail followed Boubacar, crawling between the bushes and the house. Once they reached the edge of the building, they broke cover and began to run up the hill. They sprinted through the garden, past the broken cart and the outbuildings, and over the small wall. From there they climbed the steep narrow path towards the slave village.

The moon was full, and the breeze agitated the young sugarcane. Boubacar, hearing Abigail's gasps for air, stopped by a saman tree.

'We're going the wrong way,' Abigail panted. 'We have to go get Mr Oultram, alert the militia…'

'No,' he pointed. 'If we go back that way, they'll nab us.'

'We can't leave him to fight them alone!'

Boubacar shook his head. He looked more sad than afraid. 'He's dead, Gail.'

'He might not be!'

'We should go up to the village,' he said, pointing up the hillside. 'The others will know what to do.'

'We know what to do. We need to get to the militia…'

'Gail, if I go to the militia and say a captain killed my master, they will kill me. Militia don't listen to slaves.'

Abigail shook her head. 'It is the right thing to do.'

'All Captain Vane has to do is say he wasn't there and I will get hanged for murder.'

'You won't! I'll tell them what happened.'

'Why would they listen to you?' He looked frustrated with her. 'Think. You used to be the daughter of a rich plantation owner, but after the harvest was destroyed he racked up debt. Now he's got himself killed. The house will be sold to pay the London banks. The land will be sold. I will be sold. You will be a penniless orphan.'

'Boubacar!' she pleaded. 'He needs us to get help.'

'Gail,' he said softly. 'He was dead before he hit the floor.'

CHAPTER FOUR
Escaping The Island

18 April 1718

Abigail's legs hurt. It was a steep climb to the slave village. She wanted to go back to the house, to get into her bed, shut her eyes and pretend none of it had happened. If she hadn't been so obsessed with Blackbeard and gone down to Sandy Point, her father would still be alive. She knew she ought to be desperately sad. But there was nothing. No tears, no sadness. Just anger.

Why hadn't her father denied Vane's accusations? Why hadn't he told him he would never torture his own men or steal their wages? More importantly, why hadn't he believed Boubacar?

'Stay here,' Boubacar said. 'I'll go get a blanket so I can sneak you in.'

Abigail looked down the hillside at the fields of sugarcane in the moonlight. The wet weather had passed and the moon was low in the starry sky. Below, there were no lights in the windows of the great house. The town of Sandy Point was no more than a few shacks on the shoreline. The sloops in the anchorage barely moved in the calm water. She could see the burnt-out ruins of Charles Fort and the remains of *L'Océan* in the shadow of Brimstone Hill. To the east there was a lone ship anchored away from bay.

Boubacar returned carrying a snapsack with his older sister, Aaminata who had a machete.

'You can't stay with us,' she said, without apology. 'I'll take you both down to Sandy Point.'

'Both of us?' Abigail said, confused.

'I told Nanny Inna what happened,' Boubacar explained. 'She said we can't keep you safe. If those men come for you, they could force you to lie about us.'

'I wouldn't!'

'If the men are on the paths, we won't use them,' Aaminata said.

'It will be fun, like when we pretend to be maroons,' Boubacar said, smiling. 'Aaminata knows a way through the woods and down to the coast.'

Aaminata nodded. 'It is an old Carib trail. It takes us to the other side of Brimstone Hill and down to the sea.'

Abigail was tired. It was a mile walk through thick forest to the coast, then further along the shore to Mr Oultram's lodgings. 'Why can't we rest here?'

'If what my brother says is true,' Aaminata said, 'then the militia will come here and arrest Boubacar for murdering the master and kidnapping you. Then we will all be punished for harbouring you both.'

Abigail was so confused. 'But that isn't what happened! I will tell them.'

'What if Vane is a powerful man? What if he bribes the authorities?' Aaminata said in a matter-of-fact way.

Boubacar nodded. 'What white man do you know who would turn down money to protect a slave?'

Abigail was going to immediately reply with, 'My father!' But after hearing what Vane had said, doubt spread through her mind. Rather than argue with Aaminata she nodded, and followed them both off the path and into the trees.

Everything looked blue in the dark. The only thing Abigail could see clearly was Boubacar's cotton shirt as he slashed through the vegetation ahead with Aaminata's machete. The forest was wet from the rains earlier that day. She felt her shoes slip out from under her. Her dress became torn, her stockings were ruined. When the path became less overgrown, she copied Aaminata, sliding down the muddy ravine on her backside, clinging to wet roots and branches as she descended. They travelled in silence, listening out for Vane's men.

They reached the edge of the forest on the other side of Brimstone Hill fortress, on the Phipps' estate. Sugarcane fields sloped gently down to the distant beach.

Boubacar hugged Aaminata goodbye. He offered her the machete back but she refused it.

'Is she not coming?' Abigail said as she watched Aaaminata disappear into the forest.

He shook his head, and signalled for her to be quiet. Instead of walking along the edge of the field, Boubacar walked a few yards into it. The sugarcane was tall here, it was only a few months before it would be harvested. They made slow progress, going gradually downhill, stepping through each row of cane as if it were a curtain. Boubacar was very cautious, moving as silently as possible.

Each time they pushed through the grass she expected to hear the crack of a gun, or the slobbering growl of a dog. They kept moving and by the time they reached the sand, the moon was hanging full above them.

'Sandy Point is that way,' Boubacar said, pointing towards the rocks of Brimstone Hill.

'There is a road that goes from the end of that field there to…'

'I know where the road is!' Abigail said angrily. 'Why aren't you coming?'

'I told you,' Boubacar said, exasperated. 'I don't want to be blamed.'

'And I told you I won't let that happen!' She was frustrated with him.

'Okay,' Boubacar took a deep breath. 'Let's say you're right. What do you suppose happens next?'

Abigail shook her head. 'What do you mean?'

'If we go to the militia, and they go up to the house and find Master Buckler's dead body. They magically believe everything an eleven-year-old girl says and they arrest Captain Vane. What happens to you then? What happens to me?'

Abigail blinked.

'Perhaps you'll be taken into Mrs Phipps' care, perhaps they will adopt you, make you a servant or put you on the next boat to London.'

Abigail thought of living with the sticky toddlers, of being made to eat cheese all the time and wear those awful bows that Mrs Phipps insisted on putting in her hair. And then she thought of London. Living with the grey, bony passengers staggering out of the ships at Sandy Point for supplies.

'And what will happen to me?' Boubacar continued. 'I'll be sold along with the plantation. Perhaps my family will get split up.'

'Mr Oultram…' she suggested. 'He'd buy you and then you could be back to see your mother all the time.'

'I don't want to be bought!' Boubacar yelled, so loudly that Abigail glanced towards the sugarcane fields, half expecting to see an overseer coming to see what the problem was. 'Why can't you understand that?!'

'But you're a slave,' Abigail said quietly. 'Slaves have owners.'

'Why? Why do people even have to be slaves?'

Abigail looked doubtful. She couldn't imagine a world without slaves. There had always been slaves since biblical times. Boubacar didn't make sense.

Boubacar's eyes were pleading for her to understand. 'This is my only chance at a different life. If I go to Mr Oultram's house with you, whatever they decide is what will happen to me. Right now, I can go anywhere I want. I could be like Henry Avery and make my own rules.'

'You're going to run away to sea?'

'It's a day's walk to Basseterre. That's a big port. I could stow away in a ship.'

'You can't become a maroon!' Abigail pleaded.

'Why not?'

'Because you're too loud,' said a deep voice, standing close by. 'You'll be caught immediately.'

CHAPTER FIVE
Black Caesar

18–19 April 1718

Abigail staggered back. The rich voice had startled her but the man himself was more terrifying. It wasn't just that he was huge, with broad shoulders and pierced ears. Nor was it the deep scar on his cheek or his strange clothes which were heavily patterned. It was the way he stood, as though no one else belonged where he was. He owned the ground beneath his feet. His large chest let out a laugh. Boubacar froze, not knowing if he should flee, or copy Abigail, who had ducked down with her hands over her head.

The man stepped forward, his thick arm reaching out. 'Fun mi ni apa e.'

'Mi faamaay,' Abigail apologised in Boubacar's language, shaking her head to show she didn't understand.

'He wants my bag,' Boubacar explained, offering it to him.

'A dupe,' the man said, and took Boubacar's snapsack.

Boubacar gave Abigail a knowing look. He lay flat on the floor, and signalled for her to kneel. She immediately realised what he wanted. Last year he had taught her Yoruba so they could surprise a group of slaves. They had laughed so hard when they greeted them in the traditional way. She dropped to her knees.

'O dara lati pade rẹ,' she half whispered.

At this, the man looked at her, dumbfounded.

'Eyi jẹ iyalẹnu. Ṣe arabinrin rẹ ni bi?' He asked Boubacar.

Abigail didn't know what it meant but Boubacar stood back up and shook his head. 'Rara, sir.'

The man looked more confused and looked back to Abigail, 'You speak my language? Ṣe o sọ Yorùbá?'

'Mo le so die die,' she replied, trying to say that she only knew a small amount and pinching her fingers together to show how little she knew.

Boubacar agreed. 'Die die!'

The man laughed again. 'Ki ni oruko e?'

'Oruko mi ni Boubacar…' Boubacar said. 'Jowo sir, se o le so oruke e fun mi?'

The man grinned. 'Caesar. They call me Black Caesar. I'm delighted to meet you.'

He held out the largest hand that Abigail had ever seen. Boubacar shook it and then Caesar reached over and gently kissed the back of her hand.

'Innde am Abigail,' said Abigail, mixing up her languages.

'Come, let's get warm,' Caesar said. He swung the bag over his shoulder and walked up the shore.

Boubacar and Abigail followed him. They were surprised to find that there was no one else there, just an empty rowing boat on the sand, a bottle of wine and the dying embers of a bonfire.

Caesar threw some driftwood on the fire. Once the flames were large enough to cast a light, he emptied out the sack onto the sand.

'No money?' he said, rifling through the clothing. 'You're the worst maroon I've ever met.'

'He's not a maroon!' Abigail said hotly. 'He's my slave and he's coming with me.'

Boubacar ignored her and fired questions at Caesar. 'Is that your sloop anchored offshore? Are you staying here long? Can I come with you? Can you ask your captain?'

The man laughed again. 'I am captain. What makes you think I wouldn't hand you back to your real master for a large reward?'

'My master is dead,' he said.

Caesar raised his eyebrows. 'And you both killed him?'

'No!' Abigail said, outraged.

'Charles Vane killed him.'

'Vane's here?' Caesar sounded shocked. 'Was that *Lark* in the anchorage?'

'His sloop is called *Ranger*,' Abigail said. 'He said he was a privateer. He showed Mr Oultram his pardon.'

'A pardon?' Caesar looked confused.

'We need to tell Mr Oultram to arrest him,' Abigail said.

Caesar took a swig of wine. 'Tell me, little woman. Does Charles Vane strike you as a man who would allow himself to be captured?'

She shook her head.

'Then think about what would happen to anyone sent to arrest him.'

Abigail pictured herself walking to Mr Oultram's house, him still in his nightgown, waking the militia by sounding the warning bell, collecting guns, marching with the volunteers up to her father's house... and meeting Vane, his sword already bloody, his men at his shoulder. She imagined the fight that would ensue. She would be responsible for all of their deaths. She fell quiet.

Boubacar piped up. 'Can I join your crew?'

'It's not up to me.'

'But you're the captain...'

'We vote for new crew,' Caesar said, indicating out to sea. 'It's them you must convince.'

The children squinted at the sloop anchored at sea. It wasn't large. It was probably only big enough to hold four guns. A small light was visible on deck. The St George's Cross was hard to make out in the moonlight.

'You're African but your flag is English,' Abigail said.

'There aren't any African flags, you blunderbuss,' Boubacar scoffed.

'But why not the King's colours?' Abigail asked pointedly.

'Other than Thatch, there's only one king I recognise. Me.'

'Thatch?' Abigail's ears pricked up. 'Do you know Blackbeard?'

'More famous than Philip of Spain. He is my commodore.'

'You're pirates!' Boubacar exclaimed.

'If you say so.' Caesar shrugged.

'Vane said he hunts pirates,' Abigail warned. 'Wouldn't you be safer aboard your ship?

'The first rule of piracy is to watch what a man does, rather than listen to what he says,' Caesar said. 'Seems to me he's more likely to attack plantation owners than his pirate brethren.'

'Oh please,' Boubacar tried again. 'Take me with you. Mo sọ Yoruba. I work hard.'

Caesar shook his head.

'What if I came too?' Abigail said.

'What makes you special?'

'I know Dutch, French and a bit of Spanish. A don wolwa Fulfulde naa?'

'She asked you if you speak my mother's language,' Boubacar explained. 'And I can read and do accounts. I was being trained as a merchant.'

'But you're no sailors.' Caesar scoffed. 'At dawn, I will take you to the ship. Let the crew decide. But they will say no. We can't have a woman, even a young one, on a ship.'

With that, he finished his wine and lay down next to the fire. The children sat in silence, looking at the embers.

'You can still go back to the town,' Boubacar said.

'I want to go with you,' she said softly. 'I don't want to be a babysitter or a maid or sent to London.'

His smile turned into worry. 'If they won't let us join the crew, maybe we could ask them to take us away from the island?'

'We could still join their crew.'

'How? They won't let women join.'

'So, I won't be a woman. Do you have the machete?' Abigail asked.

Boubacar pointed to the contents of his snapsack scattered on the sand, 'under my field clothes.'

'Is it sharp enough to cut hair?'

Abigail's transformation from plantation owner's daughter to orphan ship's boy took moments. Boubacar tied her hair into several small tails and, using the blade of his machete

against a driftwood log, he carefully
each length. Abigail's hair wasn't as short
Boubacar's and she could still tie it back, but
according to Boubacar, it made her look more
boyish.

Abigail had never worn breeches before. She
loved the freedom they gave her, but they had
no attachment for her torn muddy stockings, so
those had to come off. As did her feminine shoes.
She only had a string belt, and the shirt was rough
against her back.

She spread her toes in the sand and smiled. It
was odd, being able to lift her legs up and throw
her arms back without fabric holding her in
position.

'What do we do with the dress?' Boubacar asked.

'Burn it,' Abigail said. 'It will keep us warm.'

The flames rose and smoke billowed. The
dress crumpled down into the ash. The children
curled up, opposite Caesar, sharing the snapsack
as a pillow.

***

Abigail was woken by a brown pelican trying to eat her head. The ambitious bird was clapping its enormous fishy beak over her face. She screamed, which woke Boubacar. The pelican waddled away, clacking its beak with its wings out wide.

After shooing the pelican away, she automatically looked for her parasol. She felt nervous when she realised it wasn't there. Then she remembered, touching her shortened hair, and looking down at her tatty workman's breeches.

Boubacar approached the sleeping pirate, touching the man's enormous hands with trepidation. Caesar groaned and rolled over towards them, opening an eye. He did a double take when he saw Abigail.

'How much did I drink?' He got up and stretched. With a knowing smile and a wink, he reached over and tousled Abigail's hair. 'I swear last night you were a girl child.'

His gentle playfulness instantly soothed Abigail and she felt more confident in her disguise.

'You said you'd ask the crew if we could join,' Boubacar reminded him.

'I did…'

'And you said you know Blackbeard,' Abigail prompted.

Caesar looked down at her curiously. 'Mo ṣọ pe. Do you want to meet him?'

Abigail nodded. A fantasy played out in her mind of handing Blackbeard over to Mr Oultram at the tip of her sword.

Caesar waved towards his ship in the bay and started to push the jolly boat out into the water. The sea soaked his clothes but he made no effort to keep them dry. Boubacar waded out to the side of the boat. Abigail followed, carefully avoiding the dark rocky patches beneath.

The sea was surprisingly warm compared to the cool morning air. Abigail had always been warned about the danger of the water. People said it could shock you into paralysis or turn you mad. But it felt lovely. By the time she reached the boat she was waist deep. Boubacar offered her his hand and she kicked her legs and flopped inside.

The boat was kitted with supplies. Three hogshead barrels, a sack of yams, fruits and some guns. Abigail hadn't seen them last night. She wondered how Caesar had got them. He was trickier than he seemed.

It wasn't a long journey to the sloop. Her one large mast raked backwards towards the stern, like a tree bending in the wind. The enormous bowsprit was nearly the length of the boat. She resembled a tattered hummingbird. As they neared, Abigail saw her name in flaking paint: *Salt Pig*.

They were waved in by a man on deck. The children climbed up the ladder while Caesar tied up the rowing boat using frayed ropes. There were holes in the sides of the sloop from scrap shot. The planks that weren't splintered were warped. There were four other pirates asleep on various sacks that covered the deck. Abigail realised she was the only white person onboard.

'Get up you messy dogs!' Caesar prodded a man in the ribs with his wet boot.

It was his groan that woke the rest of the crew, who then began hauling the rowing boat out of the water. This movement roused a turkey, which began pecking crumbs off a square wooden plate.

'Listen,' Caesar boomed. 'Two boys want to join the crew. What do you say?'

A pirate who was missing several fingers shook his head. 'We stopped for supplies and we've barely enough to get us to Nassau. Do you want two more mouths on board?'

'Shut up John, this could be fun,' another piped up. 'What are they? Runaways? Brothers?'

Abigail and Boubacar looked at each other in disgust.

'We're friends,' Abigail said.

'Shall we put your little friendship to the test?'

This got the men jeering.

'How about we let one join? The other goes back to the land?'

'Yeah, keep one and kill the spare,' chuckled a younger man, darkly.

'Or we take you both back now?' An older pirate with a grey beard said. 'Last chance, you can both go back or only one of you stays.'

'No,' Boubacar said. 'I can't go back.'

'So be it! The one who reaches the top of the mast first, wins!' Caesar said. 'Place your bets, gentlemen. Two to one on the curly haired boy.'

'Boubacar!' Abigail whispered. 'We've got to go!'

'They already have the rowing boat aboard,' he whispered back. 'They'll make us swim for it. Can you swim?'

'I've never tried.'

'Nor me.'

'So we race to the top of the mast and whoever loses, dies?!' Abigail said. 'Which means, me! I've never climbed a rope before!'

'No one is going to die,' Boubacar said. 'I hope we can persuade them to keep both of us once they're done having fun…'

'You hope?!'

'Juude didi lootundurta de laaba,' Boubacar said reassuringly. 'We'll work together.'

The younger man swayed over them. 'Whoever gets to the top of the mast first, joins our crew. Sound fair?'

'No!' said Abigail.

'Aye!' Boubacar said.

The men laughed and Abigail felt the heavy hand of the older pirate on her shoulder. 'He's got it in for you boy. Don't let him win.'

Abigail looked up at the mast. There wasn't a ladder or shrouds, only the standard stay ropes to support the mast. The thinner halyard ropes that moved the sail were tied off nearby but there seemed no obvious way for her to climb up. Above that, the topsail wasn't set, and the narrow topmast didn't look too sturdy.

She was ushered over to the port side, and Boubacar to starboard. A pirate patted the stay rope. How was she supposed to climb that?

'When the cannon fires… go!'

It was a long wait. Abigail thought it was a waste of powder. They could just say go…

'Get a head start.' A man with a thick French accent helped her up on top of the gunwale.

'How?' she whispered.

'Use your feets, squeeze the rope and hoick yourself up.'

71

The pirates on the starboard side protested that 'the pale lad' was cheating. They needn't have worried. When the cannon fired, Boubacar shot up the rigging without hesitation. Abigail, meanwhile, trembled, struggling to hold herself in place, let alone climb higher as the ship bobbed in the waves.

The pirate with the grey beard yelled up to her, 'It's simple, lad. Pinch the rope between your feet. Move one hand higher up, like that. Loose your feet, not all the way! Keep a grip. Bring your knees all the way up. That's it. Now, reach up again.'

Abigail gripped on to the ropes and tried to climb with confidence. It wasn't easy, but, like an inchworm, she slowly climbed higher. The boat's swaying made her want to curl up and shut her eyes. But the cheering below made her continue. She was barely a third of the way up by the time Boubacar reached the topsail. He only had the final topmast to climb. But he had stopped.

'Ship!' he yelled.

The men below hadn't heard him, but Abigail had. She took her eyes off the rope and looked out towards Sandy Point. A ship was indeed coming their way. She recognised it at once as Mr Oultram's merchantman, *Rabbit*, flying the King's colours and headed directly for them.

Then she looked up the rope and saw Boubacar's face. He looked terrified. The moment he'd left the island he had become a maroon. It was a death sentence for him if Mr Oultram took their sloop. She felt her heart slide. Her skin turned clammy. She couldn't lose Boubacar, not after she'd lost her father.

'Ship!' Abigail called down, releasing her grip on the rope to point. The men stopped cheering. 'It's the militia!'

The pirates ran to the stern, and looked out towards the approaching danger. Caesar began to bark orders.

'Carry on!'

The pirates scrambled to action, running to various ropes on deck, pulling and tying them off. The vast gaff sail swung violently, the wooden boom narrowly missing the tops of the men's heads below. The turkey ran around the two men turning a capstan to raise the anchor. The jibs were pulled taught along the bowsprit and the boat leaned over as it began to move. Abigail clung to the rope for dear life.

Something was wrong. The square topsail hadn't unfurled. Abigail could see the men, pulling with their entire weight and nothing was happening. The young, surly pirate immediately started climbing her stay rope. With the man behind her, Abigail had no choice but to climb further up the mast to meet Boubacar on the small platform at the top.

'Move it!' the pirate said. Or at least that is what Abigail thought he said. He had a knife between his teeth.

The children were shoved nearly to their deaths as the pirate pushed past them to climb up the narrower topmast. He swung out along the yard, his feet stepping onto the slack rope that dangled below. Using his knife, he managed to release the sail.

'Tell them to set the topsail!' he yelled down to Boubacar. 'Quick, or we'll all hang!'

Boubacar signalled to the men below who immediately started pulling on the ropes. The topsail opened out like a curtain with each heave of the rope below.

They were picking up speed. Abigail's cheek pressed up against the warm wooden mast.

Caesar pointed *Salt Pig* as close to the wind as he dared. Abigail thought this was madness. It meant they were going slowly, with hardly any wind in their sails. To her surprise, even though they slowed down, Mr Oultram's larger ship, *Rabbit*, was slowed down a lot more. The distance between the ships began to grow.

The pirate above them lackadaisically swung back down the ropes, while Boubacar and Abigail gingerly followed him. The bucking of the vessel and spray-soaked rope made the decent slippery. Abigail shut her eyes tight as she slowly crept down.

She sat on the planks of the deck, examining her feet and hands. They were bright pink and blistered. She was grateful that she no longer had shoes for her feet to rub against.

The pirates were debating whether they should stop and fight Mr Oultram.

'She's slow, so she could be full with cargo.'

'Or laden with cannon,' the bearded pirate warned. 'It isn't worth the risk.'

'Every time we stop a ship it is a risk,' reasoned the Frenchman.

There was a murmur of agreement.

'We are only six… eight crew and a turkey,' the older man said. 'Who knows how many men they have. Use your heads, lads.'

'We need to get to Nassau to meet the commodore,' Caesar said. 'If we want to re-join his crew, we need to get there before he leaves.'

The older man shook his head. 'I just want what he owes us. We should each get our cut of the last haul before he ditched us.'

'Them two better not get our cut,' said the younger man.

There was a resentful growl of agreement as the pirates turned to look at Boubacar and Abigail.

'Didn't we say we would drown one?'

Before Caesar could answer, another pirate called out, 'She's turned!'

The crew and the turkey moved to the stern of the ship. Abigail kept her hands on the gunwale, for fear of being bounced by the waves and falling flat on her face. Boubacar reached up and climbed partway up the rigging to check for himself.

'He's given up!' he cackled joyfully. 'Yes!'

In his delight, he jumped down onto the deck, lost his footing and rolled forward into the legs of another pirate.

'Let go the topsail,' Caesar barked.

The sails quivered.

'Ready about!'

The large wooden boom swung low over the deck. The ship turned, the large sail filling out.

'Ease out the jibs,' Caesar boomed.

The men moved as one. They reminded Abigail of the militia on parade only there were no mistakes, or jerky movements and everything flowed. *Salt Pig* might be worse for wear and her crew unkempt, but she moved like she was a sea bird, gliding over the ocean surface.

Abigail found it hard to share Boubacar's delight at being on board. St Christopher's Island became steadily smaller. None of it felt real; it was all too fantastical to be true.

This time yesterday she had a home, nice clothes, pretty hair and a father who treated her as a prized possession. Now she was an orphan. She was stuck on a tatty ship with a maroon slave and a crew of pirates who had all but promised to murder her. The only reason she was still alive was that they were easily distracted.

After a couple of hours, they had moved into deeper water and the waves were long and undulating. Two crewmen fell asleep on the sacks on the deck. The young one had gone below while the old man and one other watched the horizon intently. Caesar, after a time in his cabin, also came out to stare at the horizon.

'Where are you taking us?' she asked him as he came close to her.

'Nassau.'

'Is that a real place?' Boubacar came over, gripping onto the gunwale. It was amazing to Abigail how Caesar stood so still as the deck moved, while she and Boubacar had to hold onto something.

'Why wouldn't it be real?'

'That's where Henry Avery hid from being captured,' Boubacar explained. 'I always thought it was make-believe. Like Sherwood Forest.'

Caesar shrugged. 'The British left it undefended and Ben Hornigold took it.'

'Hornigold?' Abigail echoed, remembering what Mr Oultram had said. 'He's like Blackbeard, isn't he?'

'He used to be.' Caesar looked down at her. 'Why are you so interested in Blackbeard?'

'He destroyed our harvest,' Boubacar said.

'And I want to kill him,' Abigail said.

Caesar laughed. 'I'm going to enjoy watching you try.'

CHAPTER SIX

The Voyage to Nassau

20 April–27 April 1718

After a day at sea, Abigail began to feel less disgusted by life on *Salt Pig*. From seeing a rat scuttle over a sleeping pirate to treading barefoot in turkey droppings, it was all becoming familiar. Dare she think, comfortable?

The latrine was clean, even though each time she went she risked being lost overboard. There was a little ledge with a hole in it on one side of the bowsprit that she lowered herself on. It was an amazing place to sit and watch the ocean, but not when the waves were trying to buck her into the water, or rise up to drench her. At night she couldn't be sure of her footing. If she fell in, no one would notice her missing.

Caesar was determined to get to Nassau as fast as he could, casting anything they didn't need into the sea. Spare flags, the cannon and frayed ropes were rolled overboard.

Abigail and Boubacar were put to work pumping bilge water, which was a slow process as the pump was broken and they had to do the job by bucket.

'First day's work you've done in your life,' Boubacar chuckled but, on seeing Abigail struggle, he stopped his jibes. 'If you hold it underneath, it's easier.'

'Why does it smell so bad?' she gasped, emptying the bucket into the sea.

'It doesn't smell bad enough,' John said. 'Too much seawater is leaking in. We better get to Nassau before we end up at the bottom.'

Confusingly, two of the pirates were called John and another was Jean. The Johns were maroons from Jamaica, one called Big and the other Little. Jean was a free black man from Martinique. He spoke French and taught Abigail some excellent swear words. Stephan was the younger crew member, and most nimble.

Her favourite was Bill. He was the pirate with the grey beard. He'd been at sea since he was a boy and his accent sounded more Cornish than African. He entertained the children with his tales.

'The North is but a desolate waste of ice, which even the constant beams of the sun for six months in the year cannot melt,' he said, his clay pipe lodged in his teeth.

'Constant sun?' Boubacar asked, his mouth agape.

'Oh aye, there be night. For in the winter, you can't see the sun at all. The sky be as dark as my forearm.'

Abigail wanted to hear the tales of the pirates, particularly any story about Blackbeard. Bill didn't disappoint.

'Edward Thatch was a cunning pirate and now he's a shrewd captain. He has the undying loyalty of his crew. They're mostly the cargo from slave ships,' Bill said knowingly. 'Even ones he casts off, like Black Caesar, are loyal to him.'

'Caesar was part of Blackbeard's crew?'

'We all were. Till Blackbeard and Caesar had a quarrel. Then he dumped us on this shot up vessel. Our captain thinks if we can get to Nassau before he leaves, we have a chance of re-joining Blackbeard's crew.'

'Why does he want to re-join when Blackbeard abandoned you?'

'Blackbeard is a great captain. He breaks bread with us. He even does menial chores. Most white men get us to do the worst jobs like paying the devil.'

Boubacar saw Abigail's horrified face and explained. 'The devil is the longest seam of the ship. It's just an expression for when you reseal it.'

'Horrid job – that's why it's called the devil.' Bill smiled. 'I've seen Thatch myself, doin' all manner of caulking, patching, scrubbing… He doesn't see himself above no one, except anyone working for the crown. Last we heard, he was off the Cape of Delaware. He held up a ship and made the crew watch as he took everything they owned and cast it into the deep.'

'He did that to us too!' Abigail said. 'Burned our harvest, for no reason at all!'

'He has cost the crown more than an entire war with Spain!'

'You exaggerate, you long-seed,' Caesar said, slapping him on the back.

When it wasn't his turn on watch, Bill didn't go down into the hold to sleep but taught Abigail and Boubacar the ropes, their names and what each one did. Soon they were helping haul the sails, and set the jibs.

'We have to make a stop,' Jean said to Caesar the next day. 'We have no more hard tack.'

Hard tack was a biscuit that you dropped into stew. It made a small amount of food go a lot further as it absorbed all the juices, swelling up into a fluffy dumpling.

Caesar swore.

'How much other food do we have?' Boubacar asked.

Neither man seemed to know.

'Stephan's got a line for fish. We might get lucky,' Bill said.

'I'll do a stock check,' Boubacar said happily. 'I've done loads on the plantation. I'll run through what we've got and see if we can't stretch it further. Do we have any parchment?'

Caesar nodded. 'Very well. But I'm not stopping. I cannot risk Thatch leaving before we get there. *Salt Pig* is a much smaller ship. We are slower than he is, so this is our only chance to catch up with him.'

'Why did Blackbeard leave you all behind?' Abigail asked.

'He got it into his head that I wanted to be commodore.' Caesar grunted. 'Told me he would give me a ship and left me this wreck.'

'Why did he think you wanted to be commodore?'

'Because I *do* want to be commodore.' Caesar smiled. 'But I wasn't going to kill him for it. I wanted to take over from him, if he retires.'

'Can pirates retire?'

'First rule of piracy is we can do anything we like,' Caesar said with a smile.

'I thought the first rule of piracy was to watch what a man does?'

'Scrap that. The first rule of piracy is to never question your captain.'

'Good news is the water isn't too stale.' Boubacar returned, grinning from ear to ear. 'And we've got a sack of rice on deck. Jean was using it as a bed.'

'No one knows how to cook rice,' Caesar said. 'We only use biscuits.'

'I know how to cook rice,' Boubacar said happily.

Abigail spent the next hour washing rice in seawater under Boubacar's instructions, then adding it and some green barrel water to the stew. The stew was in a pot that dangled over a low fire in a sand-filled metal oven near the bow of the ship.

Everyone enjoyed the rice, and Abigail was amazed at the stew. It was heavily spiced and, although there was no meat, it tasted incredible. Her mouth continued to prickle with flavour an hour after eating. Boubacar became quite the hero.

On the third day, Abigail was on watch, which meant she had to call out if there were storms approaching. She was under the false impression that where the boat was pointing was where it was going. She was taken aback when a squall that had been off in the distance seemed to overcome the ship within a few minutes. This caused chaos as they tried to let loose the sails and clew the topsail to stop the ship being dragged off course by the wind.

Once the rig was safe and her watch was over, Caesar showed her how to collect the rainwater by using the jibsail as a catch. Water was always running low. They made tea in the mornings, boiling a large pot over the tiny fire and adding various leaves, but aside from that and the stew, there was nothing else to drink other than stale water, red wine or neat rum.

'I'm not drinking that,' Boubacar said. 'God doesn't permit it.'

'What happens at sea, God allows just fine,' John said, and offered his cup to Abigail. 'It will put hairs on your chin.'

Abigail didn't see that as much of a motivation.

'Come on lad,' Bill said. 'It won't kill you. Down the hatch.'

Abigail did as she was told and immediately wanted to be sick. Rum reminded her of the vinegar for the pickles in Nanny Inna's kitchen, only much stronger. She thought it had burnt right through her throat.

The pirates, satisfied that the new recruit was suitably corrupted, carried on their conversation around her. Boubacar joined in. Abigail sat quietly, unable to focus as the rocking of the boat made her head spin.

She got up and peered over the gunwale. No islands were visible, the stars were just coming out, the moon and sun shared a sky. Only wisps of clouds and a purple, undulating ocean.

'You being sick?' It was Boubacar.

'No,' she said. 'I don't like rum though.'

'I don't think any of them do. They just like looking tough.'

'They aren't like how I imagined pirates.'

'They're just sailors,' Boubacar agreed.

'What are we going to do when we reach Nassau?' Abigail asked.

'We can work that out when we get there.'

'What about Blackbeard?' she whispered.

He looked confused. 'What about him?'

She took a large gulp of sea air. 'Mr Oultram said no one can catch him. No one is even trying.'

Boubacar looked confused. 'Gail. He's the most bloodthirsty pirate there has ever been.'

'Exactly. He destroyed our life.'

Boubacar shook his head. 'You're just a little girl. You can't do anything.'

'Watch me,' Abigail said.

'That's the rum talking,' he said, laughing.

CHAPTER SEVEN

The Governor
of Nassau

27 April 1718

After hearing Nassau was the new Madagascar (where the great Henry Avery had made his pirate kingdom), Abigail wasn't sure whether she expected a jungle, a fortress or a palace. What she hadn't expected was to smell it before she saw it.

They rounded the coast of Hog's Island. The low-lying stretch of grey rock was covered in the carcasses of ships, some still with their rigging and expensive cannon unplundered. As Abigail looked into the crystal water, schools of fish danced in and out of capsized boats and broken masts. Caesar knew this area well and deftly avoided the sand banks.

When they reached the end of Hog's Island they turned and Abigail was faced with the largest anchorage she had ever seen. A great black flag waved from the square fort to the west. The water between Hog's Island and Nassau was crammed with ships. There were canoes on the palm-lined shore, frigates just feet from each other and vast square-rigged vessels that loomed like flamingos among gulls.

'She's still here!' exclaimed Caesar.

Queen Anne's Revenge sat in the centre of the anchorage. *Salt Pig* slowly slipped between the dozens of different sized anchored ships and Abigail scanned the towering galleon for signs of Blackbeard. There were only a few men on guard. They waved when they saw Caesar.

Abigail couldn't believe that only four days ago she had never climbed a rope. Now she was

Jean pulled Abigail away. 'Be very careful; that dog bites.'

'He's never bitten me,' Molly said, patting him.

'Why do you call him the governor?' asked Abigail.

The dog growled at Big John who backed out of the doorway.

'He is named after Thomas Walker, who made himself governor until we drove him out.' Jean grinned. 'So, if a magistrate asks... you can say, "It is God's honest truth that I saw Governor Walker happily going about his business in Nassau."'

'He needs a clean,' Abigail said.

'You want to give him a bath?' Caesar asked, as the dog stared threateningly at Jean.

Governor Walker reminded Abigail of the dogs on the plantation but he still had his tail and his ears weren't docked. To her eyes, this gave him a goofy appearance.

'He's your dog,' she reasoned. 'You should look after him.'

'He's not mine. Careful!' Caesar said, flinching as she held out her hand.

But the dog sniffed at her and began wagging his tail. She patted him on the top of his head, which accelerated the tail even more.

'You can't trust dogs like that,' Boubacar warned. 'The overseers on the plantations train them to attack people. They go from friendly to vicious faster than a twitch of a mule's ear.'

The dog took him speaking as an opportunity to sniff him. Boubacar froze but Governor Walker panted happily.

'It seems he doesn't mind women or boys,' Molly said, also petting him on the head.

'Or me,' Caesar grinned.

'I always said you were a boy at heart,' Molly beamed.

'Well I never,' Big John said, creeping back through the doorway.

Governor Walker didn't care for the interruption and turned like a whip, snarling at Big John. The large man bolted with Governor Walker giving chase.

'Will he be alright?' Abigail asked.

'The dog will be!' Molly looked down at Abigail. 'You need a clean more than the mutt does.'

Her eyes then rested on Boubacar. She paused. Then she pointed her finger at Caesar.

'Is he your son?!'

Caesar held up his hands in surrender. 'Of course not!'

'You just picked him up out of the goodness of your heart? Whose is he?'

'I picked up Gail too,' Caesar said, pointing at Abigail. 'You're not accusing me of fathering him, I hope!'

Molly scanned Abigail's and Boubacar's faces and pointed at Boubacar. 'Who is your mother?'

'A slave on St Christopher's,' Boubacar said. 'I'm going to go back and buy her freedom.'

'Ah, so you share a father,' she said, looking between the two children. 'Not a mother.'

Abigail and Boubacar looked at each other in confusion.

'There you see, my love,' Caesar said. 'We picked them both up on one of the Leeward Islands. They had a run in wi' Charles Vane.'

'Run in?'

'He accepted the pardon and he's hunting pirates now,' Caesar said.

'I promise you, Vane's been plundering every merchant ship from here to Bermuda the last few weeks. All the men wish they'd gone with him.'

'But he had papers,' Abigail pointed out.

'Oh, everyone in Nassau took the pardon,' Molly said. 'But not everyone abides by it.'

Abigail thought back to Vane's attack at her house and what he's said about her father. All the evil things he had accused him of. If Vane was lying about being a privateer, then could he also be lying about all that terrible stuff her father had done?

Big John popped back in the doorway. 'Captain, the commodore is on the prom.'

Caesar replaced his hat and swept out of the door. Abigail, Boubacar and the rest of the crew followed. A group of men swarmed around a tall figure on the wharf. As they got closer, Abigail's heart raced. In her mind she was crouching by the wall on Brimstone Hill, a telescope to her eye, seeing the legendary Blackbeard on the deck of his ship. It was the same man who stood laughing at his friend who had blood dripping from his sleeve.

'They've caught the dog.' Boubacar pointed.

A pirate sat astride the dog holding him by the scruff. Another attempted to put a rope around the dog's head. Governor Walker wasn't having any of it and growled, trying to whip his head out from the man's grip. However, the rope was past his jaws. They tied the other end of the rope to an abandoned swivel cannon and backed away before the dog could snap at them. Governor Walker lunged at his assailants. The cannon moved a few inches, making a bell like sound against the cobbles. He tried again. Exhausted, he stopped and chewed at the rope to try to free himself.

'Captain Thatch!' Caesar called, careful to stay out of range of Governor Walker. He swept off his hat and bowed.

'Black Caesar! How did you get here so fast? I thought we left you with naught but a half-scuttled sloop?'

'She's anchored by Potter's Cay.'

Blackbeard's eyebrows disappeared up behind the rim of his hat. 'Impressive.'

'My crew and I were hoping you'd reconsider.' Caesar held out his hands. 'We have been through so much, you and I. When you're not around, life is plain. Nothing shines. What is the point of adventures if I can't share it with my best friend? You called me brother.'

'You want to be commodore,' Blackbeard said. 'What sort of fool would I be keeping you close?'

'I'd like to be commodore one day, but not while you're still around!'

'And where might I be going? Were you planning to dispatch me?'

'No!' Caesar looked around at the pirates for support. 'Ask any man! I would do anything to be back on board *Queen Anne's Revenge*.'

'I need proof.'

'Anything.'

'That dog you like so much. Kill it.'

Caesar let out a bark of laughter.

'You can't do that!' Abigail said.

Governor Walker stopped chewing on his rope to see why everyone was staring at him.

'You don't change, do you Thatch?' Caesar's smile disappeared.

'Show your loyalty by slitting its mangy throat,' Blackbeard said.

Caesar sighed. He drew his cutlass and walked towards Governor Walker.

The dog let out a whine. Abigail wanted to stand in front of Governor Walker but she was frozen to the spot. She remembered her father, staring at Charles Vane in the dining room at the plantation. She grabbed hold of Boubacar's arm. He was focused on Caesar's determined face as he approached the dog. Caesar lifted his cutlass and then stopped. He dropped his sword; it clattered on the floor.

'What's this?' Blackbeard's face fell.

'I will slit the throat of any enemy of yours,' Caesar said. 'I will cut down any man who claims authority over me he hasn't earned. But I will not kill an innocent.'

'It's not innocent,' the injured pirate said, pointing at the dog. 'It bit me!'

'Expensive thing, a conscience,' Blackbeard said, patting Caesar on the arm. 'Yours just cost you a place in my crew.'

Caesar's head drooped in disappointment.

'Throw that mutt in the sea!' Blackbeard ordered.

The pirates closest to Governor Walker picked up the swivel cannon and heaved it over the small wall into the sea below. The rope around the dog's neck pulled taut. With a yelp, Governor Walker was dragged off his feet, and was heading head first towards the sea wall. If he was trapped against the stone, the rope would be pulled so tight it would break his neck.

In a beat of a hummingbird's wing, Caesar scooped up the dog and threw him over the wall and after the cannon. With one fluid motion he picked up his cutlass and dived after the dog into the sea below. There were three loud splashes.

Boubacar and Abigail ran over to the wall. The cannon had sunk to the bottom, taking Governor

Walker with it. Sunlight danced on the surface of the water, spoiling their view.

It felt like an age. Then, a few yards from where they were looking, a thrashing clump of seaweed bobbed to the surface. It was Governor Walker.

'He's cut him free!'

A moment later, Caesar appeared next to him, taking a great lungful of air. He scooped up the dog and swam as best he could to the sea wall. Abigail and Boubacar were rudely shoved out of the way as the two Johns yelled conflicting instructions down to him.

CHAPTER EIGHT

Blackbeard's Murderer

27 April 1718

Molly ushered the children upstairs and into a comfortable whitewashed room with a straw mattress and two hammocks. There was a chamber pot in the corner, and oil lamps balanced on a trunk. Boubacar and Abigail rushed to the basin of water and tin cup, each taking turns to drink.

'I think we were supposed to wash with that,' Boubacar said after they sat back on the mattress.

'It tasted sweet enough,' Abigail said. 'Do you think the dog will be ok?'

'I was more worried about Caesar.'

'Strange that Molly thinks we're brothers.'

Boubacar nodded. 'She's crazy. That dress looks like it belonged to a Spanish duchess.'

'Yeah. Crazy.' Abigail echoed.

At that moment a woman walked in. She flinched, dropping coins all over the floor.

'Mother Mary! You made me jump!' she exclaimed, in a thick Irish accent. She was younger than she first appeared, probably only a few summers older than Abigail. She prised the last coin off the floorboards and pointed a bitten fingernail at the hammocks. 'One of them's mine. Also, that bag. Don't even look at it or I'll slap seven bells out of you.'

She walked over and slumped down next to Boubacar on the mattress.

'You Black Caesar's new crew?'

'Not really,' Abigail said.

'That's right,' Boubacar said.

'Are yous a walking riddle? Does one tell the truth and the other lie?'

'I'm Gail and this is Boubacar. Who are you?'

'Andy. I mean Anne,' she said. 'Brennan. I mean Cormac. I mean Bonny.'

'That's a lot of names.'

'Bonny. That's my husband's name but he's at sea. Brennan was my mother's name. Cormac was my Da's.'

'You mean your parents…'

'They weren't married. Well, me da was. He's this lawyer in Dublin and me ma was his servant. When his wife found out he dressed me up as a boy, took me to London and called me Andy.'

'You dressed up as a boy?' Boubacar grinned at Abigail.

'I liked it to be honest. Got me a bit of respect and some lads taught me to fight.'

Abigail looked closely at her freckled nose which was bent like it had been broken at one point.

'I got in a bit of trouble so I married James and now I live here.' She sighed.

'What's London like?' Abigail asked.

She wrinkled her nose. 'The cold never leaves. It makes your bones ache. What's your story?'

'We don't really have a story,' he lied.

'He wants to make money and I…' Abigail nearly said she wanted to stop Blackbeard. She quickly tried to think of something. 'I want to get a ship of my own, and become a merchant.'

Anne's nose wrinkled again. 'Good luck with that. Not many merchants captain their own ship at eight years old.'

'I'm eleven!'

'If you say so. Well, I can help at least one of you then,' Anne said cheerfully. 'How are you at being sneaky?'

It turned out that Anne had a side business as an apothecary. She sold pirates a medicinal powder.

'Tis valuable,' she said, 'but only a man called Raynes is allowed to sell it. He has monopoly. So don't let him catch you.'

'What is it?' Boubacar asked.

'It is crushed up blister bugs,' she said happily. 'It's like a love potion. It makes the men feel more confident.'

'They take it themselves?'

'Yeah, you mix it with food, but be really careful. If you take too much your skin blisters and if you take a whole pouch it'll kill you!'

'It's poison?'

'You vomit blood and everything! You'd be dead within minutes,' Anne said happily. She opened her large bag and bought out two pockets. Inside were glass vials with cork stoppers. They looked like mini gunpowder flasks. 'It is how the Italian popes killed people in the old days.'

Abigail frowned. Why would anyone want to risk blisters and death just to feel confident?

'How do we know who to sell it to?'

'Oh, everyone wants it. Particularly in the taverns. I'll give you three pieces of eight for every one you sell.'

***

Abigail was getting better at avoiding treading in the mess on the streets. The children walked unnoticed by the men who staggered about in the cool of the evening.

'How are we supposed to know what Raynes even looks like?' Abigail asked. 'What if I accidentally try and sell some to him?'

'We'll work it out,' Boubacar said. 'We need money for food. We don't know how much longer Caesar will put us up if we can't get work.'

They came up to the tavern. A pirate outside looked at them coolly.

'No trouble, got it?'

Inside the low-ceilinged tavern, men were sucking on long white pipes. The smoke made the oil lamps look like distant ships in fog.

'Here, lad,' a hand hit Abigail on her back. 'Go up to the bar and get me and my pals a bottle of rum, eh?'

Abigail turned to see a table of young pirates. They already looked drunk, their cheeks were rosy, their eyes glazed. Before she could say anything, the nearest man grabbed her wrist and filled her hand with coins.

'Go on, laddie!'

She snuck past the line of men waiting at the bar and squeezed in between two pirates who stank like old boots. She examined the money in her hand. There were at least twenty bits of silver… more than two whole pounds sterling. She thought of all the things they could buy with this. All she needed to do was run out of the tavern. No. She might be a pirate but she wasn't a thief.

Both barmaids were African with bright calico clothing and thick London accents. They were dressed up, with rouge on their cheeks and both had tiny little moon and star patches stuck to their faces. They looked so beautiful it made Abigail forget about the smell.

'Hold up, love,' one was saying to a sailor pointing at his tankard, 'You ain't getting no more till you pay your bill.'

'Oh, look at this one, Nancy!' The older barmaid had spotted Abigail. 'Aren't you a little Romeo?'

'Can we help you, sweetheart?'

She was shocked that the price was a fraction of the price of a bottle back on St Christopher's.

'Mind you don't go drinking it all.' The barmaid winked as she handed Abigail the bottle.

'It's not for me,' she replied politely.

'Oh, what a dainty accent he has. Little lord, you got to teach us how to sound like that!'

They both cackled and Abigail returned to the table where Boubacar seemed to have befriended everyone. They were all laughing as he was telling a story.

'... and then he said, I'll go and wake him up!'

They all guffawed.

'Here's your rum.' Abigail placed it on the table. She turned to the drunk man who looked at her in shock as she gave him his change.

'Yous didn't get one for yourself?'

She shook her head.

'You're a strange wee laddie,' he smiled. 'Honest pirates are as rare as admirals with a heart. Is Hornigold your captain? You vowed not to bamboozle Scotsmen?'

'Hornigold is at sea,' his friend said, leaning in.

'Maybe he's one of Blackbeard's powder monkeys?'

'Your captain is upstairs playing cards,' the other pirate jeered. 'Looking like death's head on a mop stick.'

'He's not our captain. We're Black Caesar's crew,' Boubacar said.

'I thought that gollumpus had sunk his last canoe,' the man chortled and on seeing Boubacar's angry face, reassured him. 'I like you two. Come back tomorrow and I'll buy more off you again.'

'If he remembers at all,' Boubacar whispered as they moved away from the table.

'They bought some?' Abigail asked.

'All of it!' Boubacar said. 'Let's find another table and sell yours. We'll make a dollar in less than an hour!'

'I'm not selling mine.'

'What do you mean?'

'I want to meet Blackbeard,' she said with a determination that made Boubacar step back.

'Why?'

'I'm going to kill him,' Abigail said, moving to go past him.

Boubacar put his hand on her chest to stop her. 'Gail, no!'

'You are not allowed to touch me!' she said firmly.

He withdrew his hand and tried to reason with her. 'He's a fully grown cut-throat pirate, with a lot of mean friends. How on earth do you plan to murder him?'

'I have a pocket full of poison,' she said simply.

Boubacar's eyes widened. 'You can't!'

'No privateer can stop him. You saw what he did to Sandy Point, and to that dog. Someone has to do something.'

'If anyone catches you, they'll kill you!'

'No one will catch me.'

'What do you plan on doing, holding his nose and chucking it down his throat?'

'I'll put it in his cup.'

'There they are!' said an airy voice. 'Seize them!'

The children turned to see two bored looking pirates advance towards them.

A plump man holding a handkerchief to his nose followed behind, pointing at the children. 'That's them! Louis Arot and Julien Joseph Mosiant!'

'Gentlemen,' the pirate said, looking almost apologetic, 'my captain would like a word.'

'Pardon?' Abigail couldn't hear them as a group of pirates in the corner began to sing.

It was a very rude song about a man falling in love with his parrot.

'He's your captain?' Boubacar said in disbelief, looking at the peculiar man.

Unlike nearly everyone they had met, he was cleanly shaven save for a waxed moustache. He had pale make up on that was badly applied and, like the barmaids, he had a star-shaped beauty mark on his cheek. If you only looked at his elaborate wig you might think he was a rich French merchant, but his velvet dressing gown made him look deranged.

The pirates in the corner got to the part of the song where the parrot flies away.

'Let's go somewhere quiet,' the other pirate said, indicating the stairs at the back of the tavern. 'It won't take long. He's overtired.'

Abigail and Boubacar were marched past the bar, through the back room and up the steep wooden stairs.

The upstairs room was larger than Abigail had imagined, and as busy as the downstairs bar. There were herbs and wild flowers dangling from the wooden beams that hung low from the pitched roof. Incense was burning everywhere to keep the mosquitoes away, and candles added to the smoke. A chandelier hung in the far end of the room over a table where a group were playing cards.

'I want you to admit to the crime rather than me beat it out of you,' the strange man said. 'Louis! Tu dois avouer mon petit poulet!'

'What did he say?' Boubacar asked Abigail.

'He called you his little chicken.'

One of the pirates tapped his forehead to show that he didn't think the man was altogether sane.

'I'm Boubacar and this is Gail.'

'This is Captain Stede Bonnet of the *Revenge*,' one of the pirates said. He lowered his voice. 'He gets confused.'

'I am not confused! These are the two lads we took from *Dosset*...'

'We are not,' Boubacar said.

The other pirate gently persuaded his captain. 'Those lads joined Israel Hands' crew. They're both fifteen... and French...'

'Huh!' Stede Bonnet squinted at them. 'Let me see them properly.'

He grabbed Abigail by the shoulder and dragged her across the room to stand underneath the chandelier. Unfortunately for everyone, the card table was under the chandelier. He shoved one of the players aside and pushed Abigail on to the game of cards so he could tilt her back and see her face.

'Oi!'

'Our game!'

Stede Bonnet was oblivious to the chaos he was causing as Abigail knocked aside the drinks, cards and coins, trying to get away while he leaned over her.

'N'es-tu pas Louis Arot? Quel âge as-tu?'

'I'm eleven,' she said. He tightened his grip on her and moved her face around under the lights.

'Vous dérangez les joueurs aux cartes!' She gasped.

Stede looked up and noticed the card players for the first time.

'You addlepate!'

'Bull calf blunderbuss!'

'Captain Bonnet,' a cool voice said. 'Can we help you?'

'Sir, upon my word, I didn't mean to interrupt, Captain Thatch, I really didn't.' Stede Bonnet was still holding Abigail by her shirt.

Abigail turned her head to see a set of dark eyes gleaming from a mass of black hair. Blackbeard. He was only feet from her, sitting back in his chair, holding his hand of cards in his long, bejewelled fingers.

'Don't you trouble yourself,' Blackbeard smiled, revealing a full set of stained teeth.

'But Thatch, the puff guts ruined our game!'

More pirates chorused in anger.

'We'll reset it,' Blackbeard said and the crowd proceeded to argue about who placed what bets and when. Stede Bonnet had frozen in place, bent over Abigail on the card table, his hands still on her collar.

Abigail could hear two other voices at the table. They were whispering in Dutch.

'We zouden het nu kunnen doen.'

She stopped paying attention to Blackbeard and started listening intently.

'Ga meer wijn halen. Wees snel.'

One of the Dutch men left the table to get more wine.

'What did this lad do to you, that demanded such action?' Blackbeard asked Stede.

'I'm not sure,' he spluttered and let go of Abigail so that she fell all the way back on the table.

'Heb je al het poeder erin gedaan?'

'Natuurlijk.'

They were saying something about a powder. She double checked her poison was still in her pocket as she climbed down off the card table. Her shirt was soaked in wine.

'We moeten wachten, het is niet opgelost.'

The men were standing a little away from the table, holding two opened bottles of madeira. Meanwhile Blackbeard stood up to take a good look at Abigail.

He was tall and although he was as tanned as every other sailor around that table (excepting Stede Bonnet's powdered face), his black clothes and hair made him look pale.

'And who might you be?'

Abigail felt an intense rage. He didn't even know her. He'd ruined her entire life and he didn't even know she existed.

Blackbeard's brow furrowed. 'Who's your captain?'

'Drinks for everyone!' one of the Dutchmen interrupted.

People cheered and held out their cups for some wine. Blackbeard held out his silver tankard. As the wine glugged into it, Abigail spotted the hilt of a dagger glinting in a hidden pocket inside his frock coat. She only had to reach to grab it and plunge it into his worthless heart...

'Cheers!'

In almost the same moment as seeing the dagger, Abigail realised what was happening.

'No!'

She tried to knock the cup out of Blackbeard's hands. She hit him hard on the arm and the wine sloshed over his sleeve. Blackbeard, without pausing, drew his cutlass and pointed it at her chin.

'It's poison!' she said.

The crowd murmured and looked down into their tankards as the Dutchman stopped pouring.

'That's the second drink of mine you've spilt,' Blackbeard snarled. 'Grown men have died for less.'

'Ask them!' she said pointing at the Dutchmen.

The two men looked up innocently. 'I do not know what the boy is talking about.'

Blackbeard turned back to Abigail.

They were talking about a powder and mixing it with the wine.'

'He lies!'

'Jullie zijn de leugenaars!' Abigail shouted back.

'I vouch for Gail,' Boubacar said from behind Stede.

A pirate sniffed his cup and took a sip. He swilled it around his mouth and spat it on the floor. 'I can taste the peril.'

'Gentlemen, why would we poison you? What is there to gain?' one of the Dutchmen said as the company turned on them.

'The British crown is offering £100 for the head of a pirate captain,' Boubacar said. 'Any pirate not accepting the King's pardon is worth £30.'

Just as one of them began to protest his innocence the other made a break for it, running for the door. The pirates who had been escorting Stede Bonnet grabbed him.

'What's he babbling about now?' Blackbeard asked Abigail.

'He's saying it was all the other's idea.'

Blackbeard looked shrewdly at the assorted party and pointed at his would-be assassins. 'Why did you try to do me in?'

'Zeg het hem dat wij over zijn horde weten, zijn geheime schat,' one of them looked pleadingly at Abigail, wincing as a dagger pressed into the side of his throat.

'Boy?' Blackbeard leaned over so that Abigail could translate.

'Um,' Abigail looked around at the eager faces and up at Blackbeard. She leaned in and whispered into Blackbeard's ear. 'He said they heard about your horde, your secret treasure…'

Blackbeard immediately pointed his cutlass at the nearest man. 'Kill them. Outside! The rug is already wet from the wine.'

'Nee! Alsjeblieft! Have mercy!'

The men were dragged from the room by an excited crowd arguing over whether to hang them, drown them or make them fight to the death. Boubacar followed the party outside but Abigail's wrist was trapped by Blackbeard's bony fingers.

His hand was surprisingly cold, and his rough skin was covered in marks the size of flea bites.

'You saved my life today, boy,' he said, almost sorrowfully. 'That is something you're going to have to contend with.'

Abigail stared at him in confusion. Why had she saved him? He would be dead right now if she hadn't spoken up.

He sat back down in his chair. 'What ship did you come in on?'

'*Salt Pig*.' Abigail wiped her wrist on her shirt, as though to get rid of any trace of him.

It was easy to tell when Blackbeard looked surprised as his thick eyebrows rose up into his hairline. 'Word is Black Caesar used an African spell to keep it afloat. I've seen more seaworthy canoes. You won't be earning much with him. I'll have you join us on *Queen Anne's Revenge*. That is, assuming you're glad to?'

Abigail knew she shouldn't willingly join a pirate crew, and certainly not for the second time in a week. At the same time, if she joined, she would be close enough to Blackbeard to kill him. For real.

'Do you know how much my crew makes?' Blackbeard asked.

'No.'

'More in one trip than two merchant captains do in a year.'

'Can I think about it?'

Blackbeard's eyebrows rose up even higher.

***

'What happened to those men?'

'Never mind that, what did Blackbeard say to you?' Boubacar asked, chewing on what Abigail suspected was sea turtle.

'He asked me to join his crew,' Abigail said

'On the flagship? Congratulations!' Anne had been busy repairing a hole in her skirt, by candlelight, swearing every other breath because she couldn't see what she was doing. She immediately stopped and beamed at Abigail.

'Did you ask if I could come?' Boubacar said hopefully. 'And Caesar?'

'I didn't say yes.'

'What?!' Both Boubacar and Anne looked aghast.

'But it is the best pirate ship in the world. It is nearly as strong as the *Whydah*!'

'Which sank,' Abigail pointed out. 'And I haven't said no. I asked to think about it.'

'Blackbeard might think about it too,' Anne warned, 'and withdraw his offer.'

Boubacar nodded in agreement.

'I don't want to be a pirate,' Abigail said.

'You're already a pirate!' Anne laughed. 'Or did you end up in Nassau by accident?'

'My father said that you should choose death over being forced onto a pirate ship,' Abigail said.

'During the war he played pirate on Spanish ships,' Boubacar said.

'That's different. He had a letter of marque,' Abigail said. 'He did it for his country. Other pirates are evil.'

'Do you think Caesar is evil?' Boubacar asked.

Abigail was starting to feel confused. 'But pirates steal...'

'From people who steal,' Boubacar said. 'You heard Charles Vane. Your dad whipped his men and hanged them from the yardarm...'

'I don't believe that...'

'... and stole all their wages, abandoning them after the war.'

'Charles Vane is a liar!' Abigail snapped.

'It's true that after the war the sailors were out of work and couldn't get home,' Anne said. 'Where do you think all these pirates come from? They aren't all maroons.'

'Why couldn't they work?' Abigail asked.

'Because there isn't any work – everything is done by slaves!' Boubacar huffed.

'Don't shout, I'm not stupid.'

'Anyone who doesn't say yes to being crew on Blackbeard's ship is stupid to me,' he said. 'You don't even have to fight! Merchant ships see *Queen Anne's Revenge*, panic and surrender!'

'I hate him though,' she said quietly.

'So?'

Abigail's lip trembled. 'If I had to see him every day, I would kill him.'

'But you saved his life today,' Boubacar said. 'Those men were going to poison him and you saved him because you're a good person. You're not capable of murder.'

Abigail couldn't bring herself to confess the truth. The only reason she stopped his murder was that she didn't want someone else to kill him. She had been fantasising about her revenge ever since she learnt his name. She wanted to be the one to destroy him. She wanted him to know why. She didn't want some stupid Dutch pirate to get in her way.

'He's the reason my father is dead,' she said.

Boubacar looked confused. 'Charles Vane killed Master Buckler.'

Abigail shook her head. 'He lost everything after the attack on Sandy Point. That's when it all went wrong.'

Boubacar looked confused. 'What are you talking about?'

'Blackbeard changed everything. We lost everything. He sold your brother... Nothing was the same.' Her throat tightened and she could barely whisper. 'If I hadn't gone down to the dockside to look for Blackbeard we'd have never spoken to Charles Vane. He wouldn't have known my father was on the island.'

'So you blame Blackbeard? He never even met your father.'

'Don't you see that's worse?' Abigail said. 'At least Vane had a reason... Blackbeard just destroyed our lives without even noticing. He's a one-man hurricane.'

Anne shook her head. 'Charles Vane doesn't need a reason to kill anyone. He does it for fun.'

'We don't need revenge, we need money,' Boubacar said. 'We could go back to St Christopher's and buy Nanny Inna! Come on Gail! It will only be a few weeks on a ship. Please! What is the danger?'

'Other than a sea battle?' Abigail quipped. 'Or a storm? Or being captured?'

'You're all doom and gloom.' Boubacar looked disappointed with her. 'I'm still going to try and get on that ship, with or without you.'

He flopped down on the straw mattress and turned to face the wall. Abigail looked over to Anne for support but was met with a tight-lipped shrug. Even Anne thought she should take Blackbeard up on his offer. But there was one other thing that neither of them knew, that tickled the back of Abigail's mind.

Blackbeard had only ordered the Dutch pirates to be executed after they mentioned his secret horde of treasure. Abigail had seen a flash of fear in his eyes after she told him. He obviously didn't want anyone even knowing about the existence of it.

Now, only two living people knew about Blackbeard's secret. Blackbeard and Abigail. She worried that with that knowledge, she wouldn't stay living very long.

CHAPTER NINE

The Party

28 April 1718

Boubacar wasn't there when Abigail woke up the next morning. She skipped the offer of food from Mrs Caesar and ran, her bare feet dancing around the broken glass and puddles, down to the quayside. She needed to stop Boubacar from doing anything hasty before she had a chance to convince him to stay in Nassau.

She figured that he would be on *Queen Anne's Revenge* so looked around for a boat to take her out to where it was anchored.

'Ahoy!' Caesar was sitting on a barrel, chewing a clay pipe.

'Good morning,' Abigail said and, forgetting she was supposed to be a boy, absentmindedly bobbed a curtsy.

This made the pirate roar with laughter. 'We've been waiting on Bill to come back with nails so we can begin repairs on the sloop.'

'We?'

Caesar gestured behind her and she turned to see a familiar beast. She rubbed Governor Walker's head, which accelerated his wagging tail.

'He's not injured then?' She smiled, breathing in the musty dog breath.

'Just rope burn under his ear,' Caesar said.

'And you're not hurt?' she asked, scratching Governor Walker's wiry shoulders.

'Only my ambition, but that will heal soon enough,' Caesar said, smiling.

The dog flopped onto his back, rolling back and forth.

'Careful, or he'll think you own him, and you can't afford to feed him.'

'Who feeds him now?'

'He's his own dog. Follows the fishermen mostly, for the scraps.' Caesar looked Abigail up and down. 'What trouble are you looking for this morning?'

'Boubacar,' she said and pointed at the harbour. 'I think he'll be trying to get on *Queen Anne's Revenge*. He's looking for Blackbeard.'

'Thatch is in the Prince Charles,' Caesar said, pointing towards a tavern on the front. 'He's got the flux. When you've been drinking nothing but watered rum and coffee for two months, beer does funny things to you.'

Just then there was a commotion on the shore. Stede Bonnet was flanked by the same two pirates who accompanied him yesterday but this time one of them was carrying a half-dressed man over his shoulder. The man was bald, and had no hat, scarf or periwig to cover him. He was screaming to be put down.

'They found the doctor,' Caesar said.

Stede walked to the tavern and the men entered, still clutching the yelling doctor.

'I met Captain Bonnet last night. Who is he?'

Caesar pointed at a sloop of war. 'He was captain of *Revenge*. He'd custom-built her, wanting to play pirate. She even has her own library. Thatch put Captain Richards in charge of her after Stede lost another battle. He's a lubber.'

Abigail saw Boubacar emerge from the alleyway and enter the tavern. She sighed. He was going to get himself killed. Blackbeard could order your execution with a click of his fingers. Abigail worried that Boubacar mistook all men who didn't own slaves for good people.

Caesar was looking back out to the water. 'It's *Lark*!'

She followed his finger to a familiar sloop entering the anchorage.

'It's *Ranger*…' Abigail whispered. She couldn't believe it.

'Vane's returned! There is going to be a party tonight for sure!' Caesar said.

***

Abigail was used to harvest celebrations on St Christopher's but Vane's welcoming party was much more than a church service and dance. There were two bands of musicians with broken instruments and improvised drums simultaneously playing while men danced, throwing women high in the air. Drinks were plentiful but it was harder to get something to eat. Boubacar was trying to open a conch shell he'd bought from a diver. It was refusing to budge.

'Have you tried smashing it with a rock?' Abigail asked

'Then all the shell will get in the meat,' he said. 'I think I need a sharp knife or something.'

'Where is your machete?'

'I traded it for food,' Boubacar said.

'Where did all the money from selling powder go?'

'Anne took some, then I bought us that bread. I didn't realise it was so expensive.' He looked remorseful, 'The trick is to only buy local food, like fish and yams. Avoid beef and grain. Go ask someone if we can borrow their knife.'

'You ask,' she said.

'I don't speak Twi,' Boubacar said. 'Have you reconsidered joining *Queen Anne's Revenge*?'

But Abigail wasn't listening, she was scanning the party for any sign of Charles Vane.

'Are you still worried about Vane? You're being silly,' Boubacar said, half to Abigail and half to the conch who was scrunched so far into its shell he could barely get a finger in to touch it.

'He'll recognise us.'

'He won't. You look like a boy for a start.'

'Why did he come here?' Abigail asked. 'Did he follow us?'

'He's probably here because he has a ship full of loot he needs to sell, and there is nowhere for a pirate to do that without being arrested other than Nassau.'

Abigail looked sceptical.

'Why would he want to hunt us down?'

'We're witnesses! If we told our story in a court, they would hang him.'

'Everyone has stories of Vane killing people,' Boubacar said. 'Last time he was here, he plundered a ship right under the nose of the British, shot at them and sailed away with two sloops. He'd have to murder everyone here if he was bothered about witnesses.'

Abigail felt a little better.

'Governor Walker!' she said.

The dog was circling a man like a shark, nearly causing him to trip.

'What's he after?'

'He's got roasted yams in that basket,' Abigail said. 'Do dogs eat yams?'

Boubacar shrugged. 'Must do. He dug them up.'

'He did not!'

'He did. When he got to the yam, they threw him a conch foot. I wish we had a dog to dig them up back home. You can't use a shovel, 'cause metal damages the root.'

'Clever,' Abigail said and as though he had heard her, Governor Walker bounded up to them. Boubacar immediately scrabbled backwards as the dog barked playfully.

'Governor, leave him alone.'

Walker immediately sat down.

'Good boy!' she exclaimed. He panted happily, rising up to place his enormous paws on her shoulder and licking her on her cheek.

'Eurgh! He smells like low tide.'

'How did you get him to obey you like that?'

'I just asked nicely.'

'You're not only good at human languages.'

'Look! It's Blackbeard.' Abigail pointed as a dark figure moved through the dancers to sit under a sailcloth awning. He was dressed more like a sailor. No coat or hat, but his pistols and cutlass were on display.

His casual dress was juxtaposed by the man accompanying him. He had an elaborate wig and his clothes were smart, made of expensive fabric that reminded Abigail of Mr Oultram's. There was a third man who was also well turned out and had a scar across his eye. Following them at a distance were Caesar and Jean, who were beckoned in by Blackbeard. They all glanced towards the children. Abigail tried to hide Governor Walker by stepping in front of him.

'Boys!' Caesar walked over to them. 'You see the men with Blackbeard – La Buse and Paulsgrave? They often speak to each other in French. Jean told Captain Thatch you speak it?'

'Er…' Abigail hesitated.

'Tu parles bien le français!' Jean assured her before turning to Caesar. 'She does!'

'But you're fluent…'

'They won't let slip secrets in front of Jean in French,' Caesar said. 'They know he understands.'

'C'est simple.' Jean smiled. 'Go up there with a bottle of madeira and keep everyone's cups topped up. Après, you tell Thatch if they say anything he needs to hear.'

'I'll go too,' Boubacar said firmly.

'You don't speak French,' Abigail said, thinking Boubacar was still trying to get an invitation to join Blackbeard's crew.

'No, but I can serve wine, and you've never waited on anyone in your life,' Boubacar said.

Abigail turned to Caesar. 'I thought you were fixing up *Salt Pig*! Does this mean you're still trying to re-join the crew? After what he did to Governor Walker?'

'It's not like that Gail,' Caesar said. 'Thatch is the most respected man on this island. His word is law. If we do him favours, we will be able to get the supplies to repair *Salt Pig*. No one will help us if we are shunned.'

***

Blackbeard acknowledged Abigail with the smallest nod of the head when they approached the party. He held his silver cup out and Boubacar immediately reached for a gun worm that had been screwed into the hull of the upturned boat. He twisted it out and used it to prize out the cork from a wine bottle. He quickly set about pouring the contents into Blackbeard's cup.

The pirate with a scar watched Boubacar, with intent. 'D'où viens-tu?'

Boubacar stopped pouring the wine and looked up innocently. 'What?'

'He is asking where you are from,' the pirate in the large wig explained.

'St Christopher's Island,' Boubacar stuttered.

'Alors, tu as rencontré plusieurs français?'

Boubacar stared blankly.

'He's asking if you've met many Frenchmen,' the man in the wig said.

'No,' Boubacar shrugged.

'What a pity,' the French pirate said. 'He opens the wine so fast I thought he was my countryman!'

The pirates laughed and started their conversation. It was focussed on tedious tallies of cargo won and lost, and on narrow encounters with the various ships currently cruising the seas looking to capture them.

Abigail learnt that the French pirate was La Buse. His companion, Paulsgrave, had a North American accent, distinct from Mr Oultram's Boston one which Abigail was familiar with, and took great interest in Blackbeard's silver cup. He was able to estimate its weight in his hand and used an eyepiece he carried in his waistcoat pocket. It was this action, and not his wig or clothes, that made Abigail realise that all the men sitting around the table were gentlemen. They weren't from labouring backgrounds. La Buse quoted sayings in Latin. Blackbeard too, understood and quipped back. It was amazing to her that educated gentlemen of advantage would stoop to piracy. Why would they throw their lives away to become criminals?

There was little or no French spoken and Abigail was getting bored when she heard La Buse happily exclaim.

'Mais regardez, les ennuis arrivent!'

The men rose up to greet the stranger. Boubacar nearly dropped the wine. It was Captain Vane.

Vane's piercing blue eyes rested on Abigail's face for a moment, but whether it was her shorter hair, her boy's clothes or the long shadows cast by the setting sun, he didn't seem to recognise her or Boubacar.

'Good evening, ladies,' he joked, sitting on a barrel next to Blackbeard.

'I must say,' La Buse said, smiling as Boubacar filled their glasses, 'the entire town is ablaze with stories of your accomplishments at sea, Captain Vane.'

'From the stories I heard your reputation will be more feared than Thatch,' Paulsgrave said.

The men laughed as Vane told them about his exploits.

There was a dip in the conversation as Paulsgrave whispered, 'Do you know if the rumours are true? That a fleet of ships is coming from England to put an end to us?'

'We'll fight them,' Vane said.

Blackbeard remained sombre. 'It would explain why they issued the pardon. Every man wanting a fresh start has taken it. They've reduced our numbers before firing a shot.'

'We can still beat them,' Vane said.

La Buse scoffed. 'How do you hope to fight a British fleet, commanded by Woodes Rogers?'

'The circumnavigator?' Blackbeard asked quickly.

'Do you know him?' Paulsgrave asked.

'Everyone has heard of him,' Vane said, trying to sound unimpressed. 'He has a musket ball lodged in his head. He's from your neck of the woods isn't he, Thatch?'

Blackbeard didn't answer.

At this point La Buse leant over to Paulsgrave and muttered in French. Abigail heard him say that if Blackbeard knew Rogers from when they were children, then that would mean Rogers could identify him.

'It's rude to chatter in frog,' Vane said, annoyed he wasn't in on the gossip.

'Alors,' La Buse shrugged. 'This is your doing Thatch. You have become such a nuisance to the British that they are spending real money to get rid of you.'

'We can beat him in battle,' Vane said.

'A musket ball to the head couldn't stop him.' Paulsgrave adjusted his wig. 'Rogers will be here in a matter of weeks. Do we surrender or continue?'

Vane shrugged. 'If I am caught, they will hang me. The Act of Pardon only works for crimes you commit before you sign it. And I've not been a good boy since signing.'

Vane's pale eyes met Abigail's. If felt like her insides were trying to crawl away from her. He looked back at his comrades at the table. Had he recognised her?

The music from the shore started up, and a group came dancing up to them. The conversation was broken as they bombarded the captains with a sea shanty that everyone, even Boubacar, joined in. Abigail, however, remained quiet, watching Vane to see if he looked at her again.

The merry makers moved on, leaving a tray of roasted fish, fruit and yams. La Buse kissed Blackbeard on both cheeks before heading off in the direction of the revellers. Vane and Paulsgrave followed. Boubacar waved at Abigail to come with them but Blackbeard had turned his head towards his informant and patted the empty seat next to him.

'Gail,' he said, pointing at the tray. 'Come. Eat.'

She walked forward. Not meeting his eyes.

'You must be hungry.' He grabbed her hand and placed an entire cooked fish into it. It was still warm. She could feel its bones through its skin, as whatever it was stuffed with spilled down onto the sand. Blackbeard leaned in. 'So, boy, what did you hear?'

'There wasn't much French spoken,' Abigail said looking into the fish's milky eye.

'There was some; when we were talking about Woodes Rogers.' He prodded her hand and pushed her onto the upturned barrel. 'Eat!'

How was she supposed to eat and talk at the same time? She hated being near him. Her chest felt tight and she realised she was crushing the fish in her fist. She coughed. 'La Buse said that you and Rogers are about the same age and if you are from the same place, you would know each other. He would know your real name... is your real name not Thatch then?'

Blackbeard's eyes glistened in the firelight and he picked up his clay pipe. 'La Buse is a clever man. Yes, I knew Woodes Rogers. Whether he would recognise me is another matter.'

'Why does it matter if he does?' Abigail asked, finally giving in and nibbling at the fish, pulling its spiny bones out from her teeth as she went. It tasted delicious and the fact she enjoyed it made her feel more angry. She didn't want to like anything about Blackbeard, not even the food he handed to her.

'I might have a family back in England…' He waved a bejewelled hand vaguely.

Abigail thought of a table of equally hairy devils huddled in a witch's cave.

'I wouldn't want them to lose their reputation, would I?'

'Wouldn't you?' Abigail licked the fish juice that was trickling down her arm.

'I'm not a monster, Gail,' he said. 'If anyone found out I had a family they'd be shunned. The authorities would do anything to get their paws on my property. They would lose everything.'

Abigail was staring at one of the flintlock pistols that hung from the sling around Blackbeard's shoulder. If she dropped the fish, she could make a grab for it. She'd point it at his chest and fire shot into his selfish black heart. She should do it. After she'd finished eating.

'The way I see it I have two choices.' Blackbeard curled a finger through his beard. 'I either stay here with Vane and try to resist Rogers or I leave Nassau for good before he arrives.'

'What will you do if you leave?'

'Go to sea,' he said. 'Leave Vane to fight. He'll find it hard work being Admiral of the Black.'

'But don't you need Nassau?' Abigail's mind went to Bill working on the sloop. 'Won't it be hard to repair your ships without a dock?'

'It will.'

'How will you trade all the things you pillage?' She spat a bone out on the sand and nibbled at what was left of the carcass. 'Won't you be sitting ducks if the British decide to hunt you?'

'If Woodes Rogers is coming here, everyone on this island is doomed.' Blackbeard looked into her eyes. 'You should come with me, you and your friend.'

She dropped the bones of the fish in the sand and said firmly, 'I'm staying in Nassau.'

'I'm sorry to hear that. Will you take the pardon?' He chuckled to himself. 'Or rather, will Vane let you take the pardon?'

'Don't worry about me,' she said, thinking that he may have a point. While she hated Blackbeard, the idea of living in a port where Vane was planning to battle an entire fleet of British privateers, was terrifying.

'Of course I worry about you, Gail,' Blackbeard said. 'We are friends.'

If her father could see her now, being addressed by the greatest scourge of the seas since Henry Avery, as an equal.

CHAPTER TEN

Conch Fishing

29 April 1718

Boubacar woke Abigail up early the next morning and they headed out along the shore. Rumour was there was shallow inlet filled with sea grass. Conch love seagrass, and Boubacar's plan was to dive for them. Abigail thought this ambitious as he'd not tried swimming before, but he was determined.

It took them a while to find the inlet. Flies zipped past their ears. Tiny lizards scuttled to the shady side of the trees as they passed. Gulls circled high overhead.

The cove formed a little bowl. It was low tide. Hot white sand sloped gently down to the sea. They were in the right place. The rocks Abigail had seen from a distance were actually piles of old conch shells from someone else's catch.

'Careful,' Abigail said when he was just ankle deep.

'I can see some already,' he said, nervously. 'Keep an eye out for crocodiles.'

Abigail didn't know what crocodiles looked like, so she kept her eye out for large iguanas and hoped that would do. Boubacar was knee high in the water. He stopped. A black headed gull on the surface paddled closer, as if to say, 'What is the problem?'

'I'm scared I'll be washed into the sea.'

'Try going a little deeper and putting your head under.'

'I need something to hold onto. Can you find a vine?'

Abigail looked around. Further round the cove there was a crab trap which might have some rope on it, but closer to her was a yam vine. She was about to pull it down from the tree when she heard Boubacar yelling.

'Gail! Run!'

Hands were on her. A man picked her up by her waist from behind. All the air rushed out of her lungs. Her ribs felt like they would crack. She jerked her head backwards, headbutting him in his nose. He dropped her. She was so winded all she could do was crawl. She felt a hand catch her foot and the ground sped under her as he dragged her back to the shore.

He let her go when they were nearly at the tideline. She jumped to her feet, her heart hammering in her chest as she took in her assailant.

He had more of a beard now, but his colourfully patterned shirt was unmistakable. Calico Jack. He stood over her, wiping his nose from where she had headbutted him.

A few feet away, Boubacar was kneeling on the sand with his hands on his head. The white sand had great wet gashes from where he had been pulled out of the sea. There was a musket on the sand just out of his reach. Barely a few inches from Boubacar's eyes, was the tip of a cutlass. On the other end of the blade was Captain Charles Vane.

'Put her here.' Vane pointed at the ground next to Boubacar.

Abigail moved before Jack could touch her, and went and knelt by Boubacar.

'What a coincidence, seeing old chums again, so soon after I murdered their father.'

'He wasn't my father!' Boubacar shouted angrily.

'Then you better ask where that nose came from, boy. Because a snout like that was poking itself into my business throughout my time on His Majesty's ships. And look, as if by magic there is an exact copy on her freckled mush.'

Abigail and Boubacar looked at each other's noses and touched their own.

'What really?' Vane scoffed. 'You're only just working this out now?'

'We can't be…' Abigail said.

She tried to focus on the sand. His words seeped into her, filling her mind with memories. Why had her father favoured Boubacar so much?

'Of course, decent men admit to their children,' Vane said. 'Trust your dad to make a slave of his offspring. There is no morality anymore.'

'There is,' Abigail whispered. 'There is God.'

Vane sniffed the air and looked about. 'Funny, I don't see him. Or anyone else coming to your rescue. Not even your new friend, Thatch. The thing about Blackbeard is, you never know what is real. All his success, and yet he cut his men a small share from his last trip. We pirated eight hundred pounds in three weeks. He has been gone for months.' Vane leaned in. 'So that leads me to wonder, where is the rest of his treasure?'

'How are we supposed to know? We're not his crew,' Boubacar said.

'Well, if you are no use to me, why don't I just kill you?'

Abigail's heart woke up. It started beating to be let out of her chest. It wanted to run.

'Why?' Boubacar said, outraged. 'We've done nothing to you.'

Abigail remembered Anne's words. Charles Vane doesn't need a reason to kill anyone. He does it for fun.

'Oh, but maybe you *can* help me,' Vane said happily. 'Do you know how pirate captains keep their treasure a secret? They take their most trusted men to a secret location and they bury the treasure. Then they bury their men with it. So no one but the captain knows its location.'

Abigail realised that the object in the sand wasn't a musket. It was a shovel.

'It never made sense to me. How do you get them to dig their own graves when it's two against one? I think I've worked it out. Jack, you can head off now, if you like.'

'Aye, Captain.'

'Digging is tiring work,' Vane continued. 'You'd need two men who care for one another like brothers. Then, you get one to dig a hole by threatening to slaughter the other.'

He swung his blade so it pressed into Abigail's neck. Boubacar looked from Abigail to Vane. He was obviously considering running for it.

'Boubacar!' Abigail didn't want to die like this, the same way as her father, with her family abandoning her.

'Risky,' Vane said to Boubacar. 'If you run, she dies. If you stay, I might let you both live. Or I kill her and run after you. You're a fit lad, but I'd hunt you. I'd rather not because then I wouldn't find out if my experiment works. I hate digging. So get to work.'

Boubacar bent down for the shovel. He began to dig.

Once the hole was deep enough, Vane poked Abigail with his sword. 'Get in,' he said. She stood in the hole; it was only waist deep. 'Sit.'

The hole allowed her to sit like she would on a step with her feet slightly lower than the rest of her. It was pleasantly cool. But Vane made Boubacar shovel sand on top of her. The sand was heavy. Once it was over her knees, she found it hard to move her legs, and when it covered one shoulder, she suddenly realised she couldn't move her arm. This made her squirm in panic but the blade of the cutlass swung back against her neck.

'Stay still.'

Abigail tried to keep calm. Cool sand pressed against her chest where it had fallen down her shirt. She tried to wiggle her toes but found she couldn't. She was stuck fast.

Vane stood on the sand around her, jumping up and down to make sure it was compact.

'Now, dig one for you or I will cut out her eye. Not there! Closer to the sea. Faster!'

The heat was unbearable. The wet sand around Abigail turned white in moments. She felt her face flush in the sun. She shut her eyes. The weight of the sand made it harder to breathe. She knew her left arm must only be inches from the surface. Grains of sand stuck uncomfortably under her nails as she scraped. She opened her eyes to see a tiny patch of sand shift, imperceptibly, like the ground was breathing. All she had to do was keep on wiggling, without Vane catching her.

Boubacar's clothes had dried in the sun and now were wet with sweat. He kept digging. His second hole wasn't as deep as the one he'd dug for Abigail, but it didn't need to be. He didn't need to be told to get into it; he nearly collapsed.

'You see, this is what I don't get. If the captain is on his own, he still has to fill in the hole.' Vane panted, covering Boubacar's body in wet sand.

Once the sand was packed tight around Boubacar's neck. He looked around. 'Yeah, I don't think I'll bother with this again.'

And with that, he walked off. Abigail didn't try to call after him. Instead, she shouted at the head, tilted, exhausted in front of her.

'Boubacar!'

He didn't respond. He'd passed out. She sensed the danger immediately. He'd dug his hole within the tide margin. The waves were already within a yard of him. If they didn't get free soon, Boubacar would drown.

Abigail dug desperately with her fingers, trying to loosen the wet sand. She had to slowly work her arm free in tiny movements. She saw the surface sand crack and suddenly the movements became large. She'd got her arm free, but was out of breath in the effort.

A large wave came in and hit Boubacar in the face. He woke up spluttering.

'Gail!' he yelled. He was facing the sea and couldn't see her.

'It's alright, I'm here.'

'I can't move,' he said.

'I'm trying to get out myself!' she panted, using her free arm to dig out the other.

'Hurry!' he yelled.

She managed to free her other arm and tried to stand. But it was impossible. As she braced, nothing moved. She pushed her hands into the sand, grunting. She stopped to catch her breath as another wave hit Boubacar square in the face. She dug out the sand in front of her and tried standing again. Still too soon. Dry sand cascaded into the hole, filling it as fast as she was digging.

'Gail!' Boubacar yelled. 'Please!'

'I'm trying!' she gasped. The heat of the sun was baking her head. The sand kept pouring in from when she moved it out. She was in tears, frustrated, her hands tingling, and arms exhausted. Another wave crashed over Boubacar.

It came far enough up the shore that it started to trickle into the hole she had made.

She thought for a moment Boubacar had said her name again but it wasn't his voice. It came from behind her. She heard the noise again and she realised it wasn't human. It was the distant bark of a dog.

'Governor Walker!' Abigail shouted. 'Over here! Governor Walker!'

She heard galloping steps as the great big slobbering dog bounded up to her. He rushed in front of her, bending down to smell her face. His shadow was like a blast of cool as he shaded her from the sun, licking every inch of her face.

'Yams,' she croaked. 'Dig, dig, good boy!'

For a terrible moment, she thought the dog was going to run off and find a yam vine. But he understood what she wanted. He started to dig down in front of her, and was nearly at her knees when suddenly she found she could lift herself up. The moment she stood she fell over again. Her legs were bright pink and numb. Pins and needles started in both feet.

'Help!'

The water had come up to Boubacar's chin. The dog ran over to him. Abigail's legs felt spicy with pain as the blood flow returned to them. She moved each gingerly and wobbled herself upright. Her first few steps were towards Boubacar, but then she remembered the rope.

She staggered away from Boubacar and found the crab pots. Grabbing the tattered rope, crab pot and all, she sped back to Boubacar. She was thankful that Governor Walker was there. It was nearly impossible to spot Boubacar's head in the crashing surf.

The dog had dug down and managed to free one of Boubacar's arms, but the boy was still exhausted, gasping for breath and stuck fast.

'Gail,' he cried as the wave retreated. 'I'm going to die!'

Another wave washed over him. Boubacar's second arm was free but the more he moved the more he seemed to sink lower into the wet sand.

Abigail ran over and grabbed his flailing arms so he could feel the rope as the wave sloshed back again. He grasped it. She tugged. It was no good. Governor Walker continued to dig in the surf, but the sand kept falling in.

'Here, Walker!' Abigail hit on an idea and wiggled the end of the rope at the dog. He immediately stopped helping Boubacar and trotted up to her, his tongue lolling playfully. 'Bite the rope…'

The dog cocked his head and gingerly took the rope. Abigail whipped it away from him.

'You need to be faster than that!' she said and held it out again.

Getting the game, Governor Walker barked happily, grabbed the end of the rope, and pulled. He was much stronger than Abigail and nearly dragged her off her feet.

'Good boy. Give.' The dog reluctantly dropped the rope in exchange for an ear scratch.

Meanwhile, Boubacar had let go of the rope and was frantically digging, gasping for air as each wave retreated. She tied the rope under his arms.

'Here, boy! Get the rope!'

Abigail held onto one end of the rope and taunted Governor Walker. The dog's tail whipped in delight at the game, his jaws snapping in the shallow waves until he got it. From there he clung. Abigail pulled back. She held the rope in a tug of war for as long as she could before finally letting go. The dog fell backwards as he pulled with all his power, the rope went taught and Boubacar was plucked from the sea floor as fast as Blackbeard drawing his cutlass.

***

Boubacar and Abigail stumbled into the shade of a tree. Abigail didn't know what to say. She scratched Governor Walker behind the ear and looked over at Boubacar who was brushing the sand from his legs.

She had a brother. A small smile flickered on her face but a wave of questions washed it away.

Nanny Inna was Boubacar's mother. She was a slave. Everyone knew that men had children with their slaves, but it made Abigail deeply uncomfortable. She recalled all the times she had seen Nanny Inna stepping away from her father or flinching when he raised his voice. Despite them sharing a child together, Abigail had never seen any affection between them.

Boubacar was older than she was. Her father had had a child while he was married to Abigail's mother. Had she known? Did she feel betrayed? Was she in heaven now, upset than Boubacar and Abigail were friends?

Abigail took in a deep breath and blew it all out. It was all a lifetime ago. None of it mattered. She wasn't a plantation owner's daughter anymore. Boubacar wasn't a slave. She couldn't quite believe she ever saw him as one. As property. Then again, she couldn't think of Nanny Inna, or Caesar or his crew like that either. Or anyone. Why were there slaves? To work the plantation to make the sugar to pay the London banks for the plantation? Why had she just accepted it? It made no sense.

She looked over at him again. His fists were clenched as he stared out into the bay. He didn't react when Governor Walker came and sat next to him. He looked furious. None of this was Boubacar's fault. If she didn't call him brother, she would lose the only family she had.

'It's alright,' she said in a gentle voice. 'I accept you.'

'Excuse me?' Boubacar's head whipped around. '*You* accept *me*?!'

'Yes?' She was surprised at his aggressive reaction. She had expected a hug or something.

'I don't accept you,' he huffed.

'Is it because you are scared of the dog?'

'I'm not scared of the dog!' he snapped and she immediately saw her father's angry face snarling at her. 'I don't want to have anything to do with your family.'

She looked at him like he was insane. 'So what? You're going to deny who your father was?'

'Yes, I am.' He said firmly. 'He wasn't my father. My family would never keep slaves and no father would keep his own son a slave. I would bleed myself dry if I thought that monster's blood ran in my veins.'

'Well, it does,' she said flatly and then, still upset that he had rejected her, she unspooled her anger. 'You're forgetting how well he treated you. It would have looked very bad if he had freed you, then everyone would know…'

'That he was my father?' Boubacar finished her thought and moved on to angry sarcasm. 'What could be worse than having to admit to being related to his own son? Poor him.'

'Sometimes it is hard to admit to your mistakes…' she began.

'So I'm a mistake? And you are what, "meant to be"? You're the perfect princess who gets the comfortable bed, the clothes, the meals, never having to lift a finger…'

'You got all his attention!' She was outraged. 'He mentored you! I got forced to babysit for Mrs Phipps. I could have been a clerk like you, I could have helped him with the books.'

'Girls can't be clerks,' he scoffed.

She was red with anger, her head pounding from the sun. 'He spent all his time with you. I would've traded that for anything.'

'He was an evil, corny faced shabbaroon and I am only sorry Captain Vane killed him because I wanted to do it myself.'

'Well, if you don't want me as your sister, you can sling your hook from our lodgings.'

'Fine!'

'Fine!'

CHAPTER ELEVEN

Finding Boubacar

30 April 1718

'Still not sold that powder?' Anne Bonny was weighing coins on the bedroom floor. She'd laid out a sheet of linen, and sat cross-legged next to a coin scale. It looked like a praying mantis holding out two tiny dinner plates. Anne was collecting the triangles of Spanish silver dollars and placing them on one of the plates, watching the balance shift closely.

'Not yet.' Abigail put the flask back in her pocket after playing with it. She pointed to the money. 'Where did you get that?'

'It's not mine, so if you try to nick some it won't be me you'll answer to.'

'I wasn't going to steal anything,' Abigail said, slumping down on the mattress. 'Why do you have it, if it isn't yours?'

'I'm doing the accounts,' she said. 'Caesar needs to buy supplies.'

Abigail was surprised she knew how to do accounts and felt a pang of jealousy. 'Has he got enough?'

'Ha!' Anne snorted. 'He has barely enough for a bedsheet let alone a sail.'

There was a rap on the bedroom door.

'Come in,' Anne said.

Caesar stooped as he came through the door. 'Well?'

Anne sucked her teeth. 'You've a bit of saving to do.'

His large shoulders slumped, 'I feared as much. Where is the boy?'

'This one?' Anne said, pointing at Abigail.

'He's gone,' Abigail said.

'What? Where?'

She shrugged. 'He said he wanted nothing to do with me and left.'

'He what?' Both Anne and Caesar turned and looked at Abigail.

'Isn't he your brother?' Anne said.

Abigail picked at her breeches. 'Not according to him.'

'He's all you have,' Caesar said seriously. 'That makes him family. It's the first rule of piracy, you don't abandon your family. No matter what.'

'He's probably gone to *Queen Anne's Revenge*,' Anne said. 'He was talking last night about wanting to go.'

'Aren't they preparing to sail this afternoon?' Caesar said. 'Come on, if we get to the harbour, we may make it on time.'

***

There was a lot of commotion on the wharf. Barrels and sacks were being winched down to boats as the fleet prepared to sail.

'Can you see him?' Anne asked.

'No,' Caesar sighed. He grabbed a pirate walking past and said in broken Twi, 'Ɛhe na Boubacar? He's a boy, er... abarimaa... obibini?'

The man took his clay pipe out of his mouth, 'there is a new boy on *Adventure*. I saw him talking to Captain Hands.'

'Which is *Adventure*?' Abigail asked, looking out into the anchorage.

'She's behind *Queen Anne's Revenge*, you can see her masts.' There was a bitterness in Caesar's voice. 'We took her when we were fishing in Turneffe. I boarded her first. I'd hoped to be placed in charge of her, but Thatch decided I was getting too big for my boots. That's when he put me on *Salt Pig* and left us behind.'

Abigail noticed the men in the distance climbing the masts of *Revenge*, preparing to let loose the sails. 'We are too late.'

'We can't let them take him.' Caesar's eyes scanned the dockside looking for something to help them. 'I love Thatch like a brother, but I wouldn't trust him.'

'Why, what would he do to Boubacar?' A twinge of worry escaped Abigail's throat.

Anne shook her head. 'If he runs out of money, or things to trade, he'll sell his crew.'

'He'll sell them? To slave dealers?' Abigail looked appalled. 'He can't do that!'

'He wouldn't sell me, we go back too far,' Caesar said confidently. 'But it is the first rule of piracy. Do anything to survive.'

Boubacar would rather die than become a slave again. Abigail couldn't bear the thought of him in chains. She felt panicked. She would never see him again.

'Don't worry.' Caesar seemed to read her mind. 'We'll go and get him.'

Calico Jack rounded the corner of the tavern. He spotted Abigail and headed for them.

'Caesar! He's with Vane, he's tried to kill…' she began, but before she could explain, Jack was face to face with them.

'Not thinking of leaving?' he said, his hand on his cutlass. 'Vane says we're going to need all the men we can get to fight Woodes Roger's fleet when it arrives.'

'Vane isn't my captain,' Caesar said.

'How much for the boy?' Jack pointed at Abigail.

'Not for sale,' Caesar said.

The atmosphere was thick with tension. Abigail thought for a moment that Jack was just going to grab her when Anne pushed herself towards him.

'What sort of get up is that you're wearing?'

Jack's expression changed. He smiled awkwardly. 'Clothes.'

'It's a nice fabric,' She reached out and touched his arm. 'Makes your eyes look pretty.'

Abigail watched as Jack melted. He made a sort of throaty noise.

'Could I trouble you for a drink?' Anne continued. 'I get awful lonely while my husband is at sea.'

Jack stood there half gawping as Anne turned, hugged Abigail and whispered, 'Good luck finding your brother. You still owe me for the powder.'

She nodded a goodbye to Caesar who touched his hat. Like a fish pulled by an invisible line Jack followed her, catching up to offer his arm as they walked into the tavern together.

Caesar had already spotted a jollyboat about to leave the dock. He hastened towards the sea wall, calling down to the men.

The two pirates on board ignored his orders, throwing up rude gestures and laughing.

'He's a captain!' Abigail yelled down. 'Show some respect.'

'A captain of what? A leaky bucket!' they laughed.

Caesar's expression turned sour and he picked up a discarded bottle from the cobbles and threw it at them. It hit one of the pirates on the head. He slumped and fell in the water. The second pirate let go of his oar to rescue his friend and as he did so, he fell into the sea.

'We're going to jump in.'

'What?'

'You'll be fine, just kick your legs hard.'

'No!' Abigail said as Caesar scooped her up and threw her over the sea wall.

Before she had time to take in the horror of the height, the water hit her. It was hard; it stung and filled her ears with echoing scrapes. All her limbs scrambled for something, anything to cling onto. There was nothing there. She was barely keeping her face above the water line, gasping for air. There was a boom next to her as Caesar dove into the water. She reached out and tried to climb on him. She could hear him protesting, but she wasn't thinking, just trying to get herself up to the fresh air. Instead of rising up, she was pushing him down into the water.

He gave up trying to calm her and dove down beneath her. She was alone again, frantic, exhausted. Caesar came up a few yards away. He swam over to her with an empty hogshead barrel. Abigail tried to climb on top of it, but it just spun, casting her down into the water.

'Stop, think and kick!' He shouted in such an angry voice that she heard him for the first time.

She clasped hold of the barrel. It was enough to keep her head above the surface. She kicked rhythmically and started to paddle forward.

'Hurry,' Caesar said, turning towards the abandoned boat. The pirates had ended up by the slippery green wall, each grasping onto debris and seaweed, and screaming to the other for help.

Abigail's fear had been replaced with outrage. Every wave that splashed her face was entirely Caesar's fault. She didn't even *want* to rescue Boubacar. He didn't need rescuing; he had run away! This was all Caesar's idea and she was paying the price. She shut her eyes as she swallowed another mouth of salty water and spluttered.

Caesar's arm reached out over the side and hauled her on to the boat. She was safe. She wasn't cold but she was trembling. She also realised, to her embarrassment, that she was crying. Not a gentle, elegant weep but a full blasted cry like a hurt toddler.

Caesar didn't shout at her. He didn't reason with her. He stopped rowing and stood up. The boat sloshed dangerously side to side. He sat next to her on the curved bottom, his clothes still dripping sea water. A large arm landed on her shoulders and drew her in, squeezing her into his side. He rested his cheek on her head. They sat like that in silence, bobbing up and down in the bay, drying together in the hot sun. Gradually, Abigail's breaths started to slow down and she blinked her eyes open.

He ruffled her wet hair, smiled and got back up.

They steadily rowed towards *Queen Anne's Revenge*. The side of the ship was like a cliff face. They dipped by the massive anchor chains and just as they rounded the bow of the ship to glimpse *Adventure*, a voice called from above.

'Hey, Captain! Caesar! Gail!'

It was Boubacar, waving from the forebeak. It was where the latrines were located, and it was clear to Abigail that they had narrowly avoided seeing Boubacar's bottom from a revolting angle.

'There's a rope there,' he said happily, pointing over to the port side.

Caesar held the rope and walked up the side of the ship with ease, despite having wet boots on. When he got to the top, he lifted Boubacar in a hug.

Abigail gripped onto the rope and, before she could try hauling herself up, she felt it pull. Caesar heaved the rope, with her at the end of it, up towards them. She got to the ledge with the latrines at eye level but didn't have to take a revolting grip on the wooden holes as Boubacar offered his arm.

'What are you doing here?' Boubacar asked.

'We were going to *Adventure*, to rescue you,' Abigail said.

'Rescue me?' Boubacar said, confused.

'What's all this dawdling?' Stede Bonnet's periwig appeared above them from the forecastle. 'Are you three ill?'

'No, sir,' Boubacar said, signalling for the others to follow him.

They climbed up one side of *Queen Anne's Revenge*'s enormous bowsprit via a simple wooden ladder that jutted out the side of the forecastle.

'Ah, you must be Key and Bigglestone,' Stede Bonnet looked at Caesar and Abigail cheerily as they emerged up onto the deck.

Abigail sniffed. 'No, sir, I'm Gail. We met in a public house, two days ago.'

'Did we?'

'You threw me on the card table.'

'No, I'd remember that. And you?' Stede turned to Caesar.

'Black Caesar,' he said. 'I was boatswain on this ship when we took *Revenge*. And I sat next to you on the officer's table every day for three months before I was left in Turneffe Bay.'

Stede giggled to himself. 'Now I know you are pulling my leg. *Revenge* wasn't taken. I am still captain. Thatch just has someone else piloting her for me.'

Boubacar and Abigail exchanged a glance of disbelief. How could a grown-up be so naive?

'Anyway,' Stede said, clapping his hands, 'with you two on board we have a full crew and can weigh anchor.'

'No,' Abigail said. 'I'm not crew! We've come here to get Boubacar.'

'I'm staying here!' Boubacar said.

'That's settled then,' Stede said. 'I'll go and tell the commodore we are ready to go.'

'Caesar!' Abigail turned to him. 'Tell Boubacar we have to go.'

'I said you should stick together,' Caesar said. 'I never said where.'

'But I don't want to be a pirate!'

'I can't repair *Salt Pig* without money,' Caesar said.

'We can't rescue Nanny Inna without money either,' Boubacar reasoned.

'I don't want to be on the same ship as Blackbeard,' Abigail hissed.

'I don't want to be on the same island as Charles Vane!' Boubacar said.

'Good to know you two are back to normal.' Caesar smiled and walked down the forecastle, slapping the backs of the crew who greeted him.

CHAPTER TWELVE
Queen Anne's Revenge

31 April–22 May 1718

Caesar told Abigail she was too slight to haul the sails on a ship this big. It took at least three men on each brace to adjust the yards. Some of the ropes were as thick as her arm. Boubacar made a point of joining in. He seemed determined to show her how unlike her he was. Everything was huge. The black flag, ready to fly when they spotted a victim, was nearly the size of *Salt Pig*'s topsail. There were three masts and pirates who never seemed to come down to the deck. They were like tiny velvet monkeys up in the treetops. They even took their meals up there. One of the children's tasks was to haul up water, rum and a bucket of stew to them every few hours.

The cook controlled every morsel of ingredients in the galley. Boubacar was tasked with keeping an inventory, updating a list of measures and weights after every meal. The food was incredible. Even the hard tack, once left to soak in the spice rich stock, tasted delicious. The only issue was the lack of crockery. There was only one bowl per four crew, so everyone ate in shifts which meant there was a lot of cleaning to be done.

Boubacar's attempts to avoid Abigail were thwarted when they were ordered to be pot washers. Boubacar still tried to avoid Abigail, choosing to haul sea water when she was scrubbing or start scrubbing when she decided to fetch water. Abigail made sure not to collect sea water when the men were using the gallery latrine. There were latrines at the back of the ship, on a balcony walkway. They were only used by pirates of higher rank. The wind blew so strongly that when someone did their business, it got picked up. Standing on the gunwale of the main deck while lowering a bucket to get sea water became a revolting game of chance, with the unlucky getting splattered with dinner from the night before.

Blackbeard stayed in his cabin the entire time. Some pirates suggested he wasn't on board at all. Others said he had lost his mind and that he would fly into rages accusing everyone of mutiny.

Abigail sat on the quarterdeck watching the door to Blackbeard's cabin closely, as though she could read his intentions through the faded wood. The sea air slowed life to near perfect stillness. Despite *Queen Anne's Revenge* being one of the largest, and therefore fastest, ships on the sea, they never seemed to get anywhere. Once, maybe twice, a day a ship would be spotted on the horizon, but *Revenge* or *Adventure* would be sent after it. No guns were ever fired, no powder fetched. Everyone knew that merchant ships would give up without a fight.

On the third day, a worried pirate exited Blackbeard's cabin and made for Abigail.

'If you see Caesar before I do, tell him to jump overboard. Thatch has found out he's on board and wants to keel-haul him.'

Abigail didn't stop to ask how Blackbeard had found out or what keel-hauling was. She knew Caesar was asleep in his hammock and needed to be warned. She held her breath as she went down onto the gun deck. It stank. The men rarely bothered going all the way to the bowsprit latrines at night and would relieve themselves in bottles which often spilt or smashed. Ducking around the swinging hammocks, heavy with sleeping pirates, she made her way to the back of the ship. The hammocks were filthy too. If they washed them in seawater, the salt-encrusted material attracted more water, making them damp again. Which was also why no one washed their clothes. The resulting smell was similar to Governor Walker's breath mixed with strong cheese, stale rum and farts.

She found Caesar and shook him awake.

'You've got to hide. Blackbeard knows you're here and is furious!'

Caesar's left eye opened a fraction. 'I don't hide.'

'But he wants to kill you!'

'He wants a lot of things,' Caesar said, sliding out of his hammock. 'And he has to learn that he can't always get his way.'

He reached for his pistol.

'He'll take that,' Abigail said.

'If he tries, he'll get the contents first.'

Caesar walked slowly through the lines of dozing pirates and up onto the deck. Abigail stayed back, hiding behind a water barrel to see what would happen. The crew eyed him as he marched up to Blackbeard's cabin door and knocked.

To Abigail's surprise, instead of being summoned inside, the door opened and Blackbeard lurched out. He looked damp with sweat. His eyes squinted in the sunlight.

'Black Caesar. Why can't you obey a simple order?!' He pushed Caesar back onto the quarterdeck.

Caesar didn't react, absorbing the push and standing straight. Abigail was expecting him to defend himself but instead he began a story. 'Did I tell you about this preacher in British Jamaica? He was the worst minister on the whole island.'

'Tie this dog up!'

Caesar ignored the crew fetching the rope and continued his story. 'One Sunday he was returning homewards and he bumped into a pirate…'

Quartermaster Howard took a rope and began to tie Caesar's hands.

'Now this pirate had a peg leg and a mean eye.'

Howard bound his hands so tightly Abigail was worried Caesar would lose them.

'The pirate, on seeing the preacher, said, "Oh sir, I do like the day when you preach!"'

Howard tied his feet. Caesar didn't do anything to stop what was happening other than to keep on telling his story.

'My good sir,' Caesar said in a posh voice, 'I am glad to hear it! There are too few like you. Tell me, why do you like it when I preach?'

Blackbeard shook his head as the crew prepared to haul Caesar over the side of the ship.

'It's me leg, sir, you deliver me from so much pain.'

Caesar was pulled off his feet. 'I make your leg feel better? How?'

Just as Caesar was about to be launched over the gunwale, he delivered his punchline. 'Oh sir, when it is your turn to preach, I can always find a free seat.'

Blackbeard's face changed. He started to laugh. The crew joined in. Blackbeard nodded and Caesar was cut free. The men embraced.

'I needed you in Nassau. I wanted word of Woodes Rogers, should he arrive.'

'Sorry, Thatch,' Caesar said, 'but I'm more useful to you close by.'

***

Seeing the two pirates hug and laugh together made Abigail hopeful that Boubacar would do the same with her.

'Oh grow up,' she snapped as he got up to get water the moment she sat down next to him.

'What?' he said defiantly. 'You can't wash pots without water, Gail.'

'We've plenty for the moment,' she said, pointing at the two buckets of seawater. 'You're just being mean.'

'I wanted to be left alone but you had to follow me. Like you always do.'

'Without me you wouldn't even have a place on this crew!' she muttered.

'What's that?'

'You don't speak Dutch. You didn't save his life,' she said. 'It is only thanks to me that Blackbeard knows who you are.'

'I got here because I asked Captain Hands,' Boubacar said. 'You got here because I helped you and Caesar stow away and Stede Bonnet mistook you for crew. Blackbeard doesn't even know you're on board. You're not special. You're just a pot wash, and if you don't want my help, you can haul your own water.'

He left her with a mountain of plates and went to help the men repairing the frayed ropes.

It wasn't just Boubacar and Abigail who were in a bad mood. The flotilla had stopped several merchant ships who all surrendered without a fight. However, it was *Revenge* and *Adventure* who took their cargo and let them loose. The flagship's hold was empty of treasure, and the crew fussed that the others wouldn't share the booty.

'How do we know there wasn't gold dust? Or gemstones?' Caesar said. 'I don't trust Captain Hands for a moment.'

On the fifth day, *Adventure* had taken another merchant sloop. The pirates on *Queen Anne's Revenge* were on deck, watching its cargo being unloaded. Abigail had busied herself collecting water when a man came out of Blackbeard's quarters and marched up to her. He looked familiar but she couldn't place him. He was unshaven, with stained clothes and a face full of bruises.

'Boy,' he said. 'Does the chef have garlic on board?'

Abigail nodded.

'Fetch it to me,' he said.

She raised her eyebrows. 'The cook will want to know what it is for. I can't just steal some because you want it.'

'It is for treating the captain,' he said, aggravated at the question. 'I'm the ship's surgeon.'

She remembered the man she saw being carried into the tavern.

'You're a prisoner?'

'Yes, but they let me loose at sea. I can't escape when we are far from land.'

'But you're still treating them?'

'Of course,' he said curtly. 'I took an oath to heal people. Fetch garlic and take it to the captain.'

She went to the galley at the front of the ship. The cook wasn't there, but there was a garlic bulb, so she popped it in the pocket that hung from her string belt.

Back on deck the pirates were preparing to hoist something large out of the water. She didn't dally, and went straight to Blackbeard's door. Without knocking, she opened it and snuck inside.

The air was stuffy. The room was cast in sunlight that came in through the grubby windows. Blackbeard was slumped on his cot, facing the wall. She crept towards his desk where she could put the garlic down unnoticed.

'Take a step further and I'll gut you from gullet to gizzard!' Blackbeard's sword appeared out of nowhere and was pointed at her throat. He had sat up in his cot.

'I brought you garlic!'

Blackbeard blinked and lowered the sword. 'Gail? How long have you been aboard?'

'Since we left Nassau,' she said.

'Whoever named you Gail got it right. You're as unpredictable as a storm.'

'Do you want the garlic?' she said, reaching in her purse. Her fingers brushed against the tiny flask of poison.

He waved his hands dismissively. 'That sawbones knows it is useless.'

She put it down on the table and it immediately bumped into an ink pot that was sliding with the flow of the ship. It hadn't been put back in its holder. She was aware that Blackbeard's gaze was focused on her like a snake. She wanted to run out of the room.

'Anything else?'

'Aye,' Blackbeard said and pointed out of the window. 'There's a boat approaching containing one Josiah Burgess. He was a pirate captain but he took the King's pardon, same time as Vane. Unlike Vane, it seems he has truly turned merchant. I want you to watch him.'

'Burgess is an English name, isn't it?'

'Aye, he'll speak English.'

'Then why…' She couldn't understand why he needed her to translate for him.

'I'm addled. My mind is sliding around like that ink pot. I can't read men's thoughts no more. Burgess used to be a friend…' He sighed. 'I need clarity. I want to know if I can trust him.'

There was a knock and Blackbeard stood, his tall frame waving like seaweed in the wash. A tiny man entered and greeted his old friend with a hug.

'Thatch!' he exclaimed. 'No better pirate to be plundered by!'

Abigail busied herself with opening a wine bottle, using a gun worm as she'd seen Boubacar do before. She wasn't as strong as him and held the bottle between her feet to pull the cork out.

The flask of poison felt heavy in her purse. Blackbeard was distracted and his wine was ready to be poisoned. She should take her chance. She paused. If she killed Blackbeard now, she wouldn't get any treasure. Boubacar wouldn't be able to rescue his family and Caesar wouldn't be able to repair *Salt Pig*. If she poisoned the bottle, she could kill Burgess. He had taken the pardon. Even if he were still a pirate, she had nothing against him personally. Abigail was a bundle of indecision. So much so that her arms shook as she poured out the wine into Blackbeard's silver cup.

'You aren't looking too steady, Thatch.'

'It is the pox. Sawbones says he can treat it, but I need quicksilver.'

'We've none. All *Providence* is carrying is bottled ale and earthenware plates. We've no doctor for you to press either.'

'Didn't you hear me?!' Blackbeard slammed his hand down on the table, his eyes wide. 'I said we had a doctor! We need mercury!'

Burgess was taken aback. 'I heard you, Thatch.'

'Apologies.' Blackbeard looked down into his cup. 'I'm maggoty headed. We won't take your cargo. We'll pay for it.'

Abigail nearly dropped the wine bottle in shock.

Burgess also looked surprised. 'What happened to murdering half the crew and sinking the vessel?'

'I've never murdered a crew. I've just made them think I would.' Blackbeard winked. 'Where have you come from?'

'Charles Town,' he said. 'Carolina. Many pirates took the pardon there and stayed on.'

'Is it defended?'

'Until Woodes Rogers arrives, Charles Town is a sitting duck.'

'Good,' Blackbeard said. 'Any pickings?'

'I left two days ago and there are ships preparing for Boston. *Crowley* is to depart soon for London. I'd wager she would have medicine aboard.'

Blackbeard was staring at him intently. 'No defences?'

Burgess shook his head. 'There's cannon but they've no fort. Charles Town sits right where two large rivers meet. Five miles from the sea. You negotiate a sandbar to get in, but they've a pilot ship aiding vessels across.'

'Armed?'

Burgess shrugged. 'Not compared to you.'

'What about scouts?'

'The only souls living on the coast are flies. The surf is rough, and the estuary is shallow in places. It's easy to run aground.'

'So you'd recommend to stay clear of the town and capture the vessels crossing the sandbar?'

Burgess nodded. 'It is the only way in and out. If you control the sandbar, you control Charles Town.'

Blackbeard seemed satisfied. 'Go speak to the boatswain. We'll pay you for the cargo but you can show us the way to Charles Town.'

Burgess happily agreed. Abigail was appalled that he would lead pirates to pillage his new home town. Despite accepting the pardon, it appeared he was still a pirate through and through.

Burgess left but Blackbeard slumped back down. He leaned back and looked up at the ceiling. The rocking of the ship caused his long hair to swing over the back of his chair.

'So Gail,' he croaked. 'Can I trust him to lead us to Charles Town and not into the path of the British?'

Abigail put down the wine bottle and said, 'Why would he lie? You offered to buy his cargo. What would he gain?'

'Wouldn't leading me to my doom be the right thing to do?' Blackbeard asked. 'I am the devil of the seas.'

Abigail remembered the night of her father's death. She had decided not to wake Mr Oultram. 'Are there any British ships able to defeat you? If he led you into the path of a British ship, he couldn't be sure you would be captured. Then he would have the death of those men on his conscience and you would still be alive to punish him.'

Blackbeard grunted a laugh. 'You're astute for a nipper. Do you know how long it takes to cross the Atlantic?'

'Eight weeks?'

'We have until July before Woodes Rogers arrives with his fleet.' He sighed. 'Then there will be British vessels capable of all manner of devastation.'

Abigail took a breath. They had less than two months to get enough treasure to free Nanny Inna and repair *Salt Pig*. Then she would have to hope the offer of a King's pardon would still be open to her. Otherwise, if she was caught, she would be hanged as a pirate.

'Will you fight with Vane or take the pardon?' she asked.

'If I don't get a cure, I won't be alive to do either.'

CHAPTER THIRTEEN

The Capture of *Crowley*

28th May 1718

Blackbeard's fleet took the pilot ship near the sandbar of Charles Town with ease. At the first sight of the large black flags, the tiny ship lowered her flag in surrender.

Queen Anne's Revenge and the flotilla spent the next few days prowling the entrance to the sandbar, stopping all shipping that came through. By nightfall, *Adventure* and *Revenge* had captured two more boats trying to enter Charles Town and one leaving. Despite the growing darkness, Caesar watched closely, studying the numbers of trunks, barrels and boxes that were taken onto the other vessels in the fleet. Abigail and Boubacar stood either side of him, trying to see anything at all in the moonlight.

Caesar sighed. 'Unless those barrels contain gold dust, we have eaten more than we have taken so far on this adventure. What is Thatch thinking?'

'He wants mercury,' Abigail said.

'Mercury is no good against Rogers. We should be stocking up while we can, otherwise we will have nothing left to fight him.'

'Is the plan to fight?' Boubacar asked. 'I thought we would take the pardon.'

'I'm going to,' Abigail said.

'Even if it means turning on your crew mates?' Caesar asked.

'But you'll take it with us,' Abigail said. 'So they can't hurt you.'

'If we take the pardon,' Caesar sighed, 'They will want all the information we have on Blackbeard. And they will want paying.'

Boubacar looked shocked. 'You don't have to pay to take the pardon.'

'Authority never lies, eh? Of course you will have to bribe them.'

Abigail saw the problem. Even if they were paid enough for Caesar to repair *Salt Pig*, she would likely have to be given up as a bribe if they wanted to take the pardon. If they didn't take the pardon they would be outlaws forever.

'Ship ahoy!

The call came from above, and then another.

'Port side! Ship!'

The assembled crew ran to the forecastle to see what was trying to pass in the night.

Blackbeard marched up to the poop deck with an eye glass.

'It must be *Crowley*! The ship Burgess said was bound for London. It is sure to have medicine.' He smiled as the moonlight twinkled in his oily beard.

Quartermaster Howard started to bark orders for the men to prepare the cannon.

'They're showing spirit.' Blackbeard looked happy. 'Trying to get away. We best put on a show! Caesar!'

'Aye?'

'Signal to *Adventure* to guard the sandbar. When we're in range, Howard can give a warning shot. Tell the lads to put on their war paint.'

The enormous sails creaked as the pirates started singing, pulling on the ropes with every 'ho'. They soon made up a league on the escaping vessel. This delighted the crew who sang ever louder. The song carried across the ocean so that by the time *Queen Anne's Revenge* was close, there was no way the people on board couldn't hear the bloodthirsty lyrics.

When the swivel gun fired, the whole crew cheered and, grabbing their weapons, they ran to the port side and took their shirts off.

Caesar handed them a lamp. 'You two, light the torches.'

Pirates climbed the rigging, shirtless and angry, knives in their teeth, and torches in their hands. It was as though hell had risen up out of the ocean. They began singing a song in Twi, similar to the music Abigail had heard at the party in Nassau. It sounded joyful on the shore, but now, slowed down and with the beating of weapons and flesh, it was terrifying.

Abigail could make out the ghostly faces of the merchants, scurrying around the deck of *Crowley*. They'd taken defensive positions but were yet to fire.

Abigail knew why they looked scared. Everyone on that vessel either owned slaves or profited from them. Now they were faced with a wall of African pirates all armed to the teeth. She was staggered they hadn't surrendered already. They couldn't outrun *Queen Anne's Revenge*.

They came broadside with *Crowley*. Blackbeard swept down the steps from the quarterdeck. He'd set fuses in his beard on fire. They sparked as he marched over the deck. The ribbons in his beard shone red in the flames.

Smoke from some hemp he'd also set light to bloomed around him, whipped up with his hair in the sea breeze. His eyes were dark under his hat. He didn't look human.

Blackbeard stooped to pick up something from the deck and continued his march towards the side of the ship that was facing *Crowley*. For a moment Abigail thought he was going to jump into the sea. Instead, he leapt up onto the gunwale. He stood shoulder to shoulder with the bare-chested pirates who were still clinging to the shroud and shouting abuse at the enemy vessel. Blackbeard used the fuse in his beard to light the object he'd picked up. Abigail gulped. It was a grenade. Grenades were hollow iron balls filled with gunpowder and ignited by a slow burning fuse. It sparkled menacingly. Abigail knew that grenades were incredibly dangerous and could explode at random. Blackbeard tossed the grenade to himself a couple of times before throwing it in a long arc towards *Crowley*. It landed on the poop deck. The pirates roared with laughter as the sailors ran up to throw it in the sea.

The grenade exploded just before it hit the water. *Crowley*'s flag was lowered in surrender. They came in closer and the pirates swung down from loose rigging onto the deck. The merchants and sailors aboard all dropped their weapons.

Once the pirates were aboard, the cargo was transferred. Abigail and Boubacar helped the crew bring *Crowley*'s passengers across to the pirate ship. They had only just left Charles Town so they still smelt of soap and dried flowers. A four-year-old boy dressed in fine clothes looked coldly at Abigail as she helped him onto the deck.

'Your soul is doomed,' he said. 'I pity you.'

Abigail wanted to say that she'd once had nice clothes and parents and morals. None of this was her fault. He didn't realise good people could also turn pirate.

'Don't be afraid, it will all be alright,' she whispered as she moved him away from the trampling feet and up onto the steps of the quarterdeck.

The deck of *Queen Anne's Revenge* was crowded with hostages, handing over their pockets, wigs, hats and gloves to the pirates. Abigail joined in but didn't take the rings or necklaces she was offered. She placed them carefully back in the pockets they came in. But she did keep a small number of coins. She had to take something or else it would look suspicious. The hostages looked surprised that they still had their valuables, but they kept quiet.

'Enough!' Blackbeard was on the quarterdeck, holding something in his arms. 'You all be wastin' time. Someone here must have quicksilver. Give it up now, and I'll let this boy live.'

A man's voice cried, 'William!'

Blackbeard was holding the arm of the little boy Abigail had helped aboard. She had accidentally placed him right in Blackbeard's view. The boy was fighting to break free but Blackbeard had already tied him by the ankles and he toppled over. Blackbeard signalled to Howard. The boy was hoisted to the yard above. He was upside down but only started to cry when he was swung out over the pitch-black sea. He was dangling over the side of the ship, ready to be dropped.

Abigail's attention was fixed on Blackbeard. 'Come now, who has quicksilver? Will no one speak?' he said.

The passengers started babbling, offering land, clothing, anything to save the child.

'Mercury!' Blackbeard shouted and swung at the rope holding the boy. He cut into it, but it wasn't sliced through. 'NOW!'

The crowd stared blankly back.

Blackbeard, angered, cut the rope. The boy fell, the people on deck screamed, and then suddenly, the boy stopped, jolted as the rope became taut. Everyone, including Blackbeard, searched for the cause of the jam. It was Boubacar. He was up on the yard. He had wrapped the rope around his arm and was holding on for dear life.

Caesar bolted up the mizzenmast, climbing to reach Boubacar. He took hold of the rope, winching William back to safety on the quarterdeck. Boubacar came down from the mast, his arm striped red from the rope burn, and helped Abigail free William from the rope. Blackbeard was raging at the crowd, demanding medicines, while William couldn't do anything but cry in relief. Boubacar was about to speak but Abigail shook her head, putting her arm around the boy and letting him weep into her shirt.

Blackbeard was exasperated. He ordered the prisoners back onto *Crowley*. This triggered a huge amount of fear from the hostages.

'What do you mean to do to us?'

'We'll be murdered!'

Blackbeard swung his cutlass at the children. William stopped crying and bravely stood up. 'Go,' Blackbeard said, gesturing down the steps to the crowd. William didn't need telling twice and bolted down the steps. Blackbeard's cutlass pointed at Boubacar. 'You can join them, lad.'

Boubacar looked at the hostages walking back over the planks that joined the two ships. He didn't argue. Nor did he glance at Abigail before joining them.

'Boubacar!' she called after him but he couldn't hear her over the noise of the terrified hostages.

The hostages were pushing back, trying to reason with their captors. The pirates were pitiless. They waved torches in their faces, pricked them with their knives and shoved them down into *Crowley*'s hold. It was hard to see Boubacar in the chaos.

'Gail!'

It was Blackbeard.

'You aren't going to kill them, are you?' she asked.

'That is up to the people of Charles Town,' he said. 'Take Caesar and one of the prisoners and sail there tonight. Tell them I will kill every last hostage if they don't deliver quicksilver to me. If they don't comply by… how long should it take? Nightfall tomorrow?'

'We need more time,' Abigail said.

'Fine, we'll say noon the day after tomorrow. If I don't hear word by then, I'll cut their heads off.'

Abigail looked appalled. 'You won't really, will you? That's just a story to make them scared?'

He did nothing to ease her mind. 'You have tonight, tomorrow and until noon the day after.

Come back with the medicine or I will kill the hostages.'

Abigail and Caesar got into a jolly boat with some supplies and a signed letter from Blackbeard to the Governor of Charles Town.

Abigail suddenly had an idea. 'Blackbeard says we are to take a hostage. We should take Boubacar.'

'No,' Caesar said. 'We'll need someone who knows the way. Someone the Governor will recognise who can tell them what's been happening so they'll pay up.'

'Fine. But choose someone who isn't strong, so they don't try to escape.'

Caesar chuckled, using his oars to stop them hitting *Crowley*'s hull. 'We need a fit man who can row. We've a long way to travel to get to Charles Town.'

'But he'll be our prisoner!' Abigail said, tying the jolly boat to the lowered rope. She felt for the rope ladder to climb up to *Crowley*'s deck. 'We've got to tie him up or he'll escape.'

'Not if he cares about the lives of the hostages,' Caesar said, double checking the knots Abigail made before following her up. 'He'll want to get to Charles Town as much as Thatch does.'

'What if the hostage we pick doesn't care about anyone else and tries to run away?'

Caesar chuckled. 'You worry too much.'

Caesar greeted the pirate on the deck and told him their mission. As they approached *Crowley*'s hold, Abigail could hear women crying.

'Fish one out,' he said.

The pirate opened up the hatch into the hold.

Lifting a lantern high over the darkness, Abigail couldn't see Boubacar, just wild, frightened eyes.

'They mean to burn us alive!' a woman squeaked, pointing at the lantern.

This triggered a great wailing. Several men made a lunge for the hatch door and the pirates swished their cutlasses to keep them back. Caesar strode forward and offered his arm; it was immediately grabbed by a hostage.

'Let this one through,' he said, falling backwards as the hostage climbed up through the hatch. Once through, the plank covering the hatch was replaced with a boom, and the people below were plunged back into darkness.

The escaped hostage attempted to fight Caesar but Caesar was too fast, and pinned him on the deck.

'What's your name?' Abigail asked.

The hostage didn't answer, so Caesar squeezed him harder. 'Marks,' the man said.

'How do you do Mr Marks? Would you like to save everyone's lives?'

CHAPTER FOURTEEN

The Siege of
Charles Town

29th May–3rd June 1718

Abigail wished they'd chosen a different hostage.
Mr Marks was overly superstitious. He explained
that he had known there would be a pirate attack
because they had women on board. He refused
to get into the jolly boat without turning round
three times and spitting. He insisted on following
the shoreline which not only added unnecessary
length to their journey but also made it more

perilous. Caesar argued with him but Mr Marks was convinced that sea serpents roamed the deeper waters at night and felt safer in the shallows.

Abigail concentrated on keeping the small quantity of provisions they had, and the ransom letter from Blackbeard, safe on board as the vessel bucked over the breaking waves.

She, like the others, hadn't spotted the rocks. Just as Caesar ordered Mr Marks to let go of the tiller, a great monster smashed through the bottom of the hull. It splintered, flinging everyone into the sea.

The water roared in Abigail's ears. She opened her eyes and saw nothing, just dark purple shadows falling past her. She was being dragged backwards, downwards. Small stones and seaweed lashed her face. The moment she realised she was being sucked along the bottom of the seabed, another wave moved in, flipping her forward. The noise went from a deep roar to a hiss as the waves spun her forward towards the shore. And again, the ocean tilted its cup, dragging her back down to the depths. The sea was a cat, and she was the mouse. It was letting her go and then using its claws to wrench her back in.

She was pushed back up towards the shallows. This time she was able to control her ascent, so that she remained face down. The sea began to suck her back so she stabbed both her hands into the sand, as deep as they would go. It worked. She was still being dragged backwards but not as far. Her face stung as tiny pebbles hit it, the bubbles of water from the broken wave forcing themselves up her nose. But this time she was anchored so that when the swell came in again, she was pushed so far up towards the shore that the top of her head broke the surface. She was able to kneel in the gently lapping water.

She staggered away from the sea and took a lungful of air. She coughed. Her nose and eyes prickled from the salt. She spat and coughed again.

'You're alive!' It was Mr Marks. 'Praise the Almighty.'

'Where's Caesar?'

'Washed up over there,' Mr Marks said, offering her his hand.

'You're hurt.'

'I got cut on the rocks,' he said, showing her his arm, 'but I'm in one piece. More than can be said about the boat.'

The small boat was stuck fast on the rocks. It was eerily still, surrounded by the crashing waves.

'I was right to pilot us close to shore,' said Mr Marks. 'If we'd've been further out we'd've never made it onto land.'

'But we wouldn't have hit those rocks,' Abigail said.

'We're still miles from Charles Town,' Caesar said, coming over and patting Abigail on the shoulder. 'We only have tomorrow and the next morning to get there and get the supplies back to Thatch.'

Mr Marks shrugged. 'I'll light a fire. Someone will be along to rescue us.'

***

Not only could Mr Marks not light a fire, but no one came to rescue them.

Dawn revealed that they weren't the first vessel to hit these rocks. There was all manner of flotsam washed up on the shoreline. Caesar went back to the boat, salvaging a bottle of ale and some flints so at least they could start a fire. They cooked a meagre meal of crabs. Abigail watched the sun rise higher in the sky as she kept an eye out for a distant sail. She repeatedly slapped herself as the gnats besieged her. The air waved in the sun-like sea. She could barely see the sandbar over the heat haze.

'I've found our means of escape!' Mr Marks said happily as the sun was getting lower in the sky.

He brought them to a hatch that had broken off a large vessel and washed up further along the shore.

'A raft!' he said.

Once they pushed it out into the water, they quickly found it was only just buoyant. When all three stood on it, it began to sink.

'Mr Marks and I can swim and paddle it with Gail on top,' said Caesar.

'Now? It will be dark in a few hours,' Mr Marks said.

'We only have till midday tomorrow to get to Charles Town, find the Governor, convince him to agree to Thatch's demands and get back to *Queen Anne's Revenge* with the medicine,' Abigail said. 'Or he'll kill Boubacar and the hostages. We'll have to travel in the dark.'

Mr Marks didn't think much of this idea, listing all the potential creatures that could eat them. However, having found nothing more to forage, he reluctantly agreed to the plan.

The tide wasn't with them, and their progress was painfully slow. Abigail tried keeping them going with a song, sometimes slipping into the water to help them push. She kept look out for any sign of fires or lamps but there was nothing. Just the moon and the lapping of the water. It was a long night and they were exhausted.

When dawn came, Mr Marks was asleep with his legs dangling in the water. Caesar and Abigail gripped the wood with wrinkled fingers, slowly paddling it forward. A gull swooped down and landed on Mr Marks. Abigail looked up just as it dolloped a white and brown mess all down his back. Her laughter was cut short by something on the horizon.

'A sail!'

She climbed up onto the raft, nearly capsizing it and causing Mr Marks to slip back into the sea.

'Mother!' he cried and splashed about in panic.

Abigail jumped up and down, her soaked clothes slapping her stomach and thighs. She waved her arms, yelling at the top of her lungs. To her immense relief, two small fishing boats turned.

The pilots of the two luggers turned out to be a white man and his two slaves. The slaves manned the larger of the two boats. They wore white caps, and spoke to each other in Igbo. Mr Marks knew the other man, who immediately took him into his boat. Caesar was made to stay on the raft. Abigail focused on the other boat, trying to remember some of the greetings Boubacar had taught her.

'Ndeewo,' Abigail said.

This delighted the slaves who burst into laughter. They looked as though they could have been father and son. Their names were Koby and Uzoma.

'Call me Uzzy,' the younger man grinned.

He manoeuvred their boat so she could climb aboard. They immediately gave her some fresh water from a barrel and sat her in the sun to warm up and dry out.

'Can you teach me more. Please?'

'Biko,' said Uzzy, smiling. 'That means please.'

'What other words do you know?' Koby asked.

'Ọkụkọ?' Abigail offered.

They laughed again. 'Chicken? You not gonna get very far with that!'

Eventually, Mr Marks and Caesar came to an arrangement with the white fisherman. They climbed aboard the slaves' lugger.

'He's going to send a message to the pirates for us,' said Mr Marks. 'That will give us more time.'

'Thatch might not believe him.' Caesar grunted. 'You've sent him another hostage.'

'We need to go to Charles Town right now,' Mr Marks said, laying down in the bottom of the boat.

'The tide's against us…' Koby warned.

'I don't want to hear excuses, boy!' snapped Mr Marks. 'Get us there. Now.'

Koby and Uzzy looked worried but Caesar turned to Mr Marks. 'Count the friends you have, Mr Marks. These two men might be interested in turning pirate given the opportunity.'

Mr Marks opened his mouth to retort, but thought better of it.

The sun rose dazzlingly high. Abigail, sat in the shadow of the sail, watching as Mr Marks turned from pink to red while he slept. She prayed the fisherman had found *Queen Anne's Revenge*. She hoped Blackbeard had listened to him. She tried not to think about Boubacar. How scared he must be. How he was depending on her. Her guts rumbled but she wasn't hungry. She felt sick. She kept her eyes on the horizon for Charles Town and scratched nervously at the insect bites that dotted her arms.

They heard Charles Town before they saw it. Great flocks of gulls screamed from the docks. A huge flag bearing King's colours flew proudly from a small bastion lined with cannon, that hid behind it the largest metropolis Abigail had ever seen. She could make out three church spires above the fifty or so buildings that lined the walled dockside. Smoke billowed out of every chimney. Her view was blocked by the masts of dozens of vessels on the quayside.

Their small sail boat slunk in between the larger vessels on Smith's Quay. Caesar handed Abigail the rope. She jumped onto the wooden planks and heaved the lugger to. She loosely tied it off and waited for Caesar and Mr Marks to follow.

The docks were crowded local produce heading out for export. Instead of the sugar Abigail was used to, there were barrels of rice and crates of wild animal hides. The majority of people were slaves but there were plenty of free dockers and merchants too. There were men on horses and there were carts of sacks pulled by mules. Koby spoke to Caesar very quickly in Igbo and then, after seeing some militiamen marching towards them, he and Uzzy made a fast departure.

Abigail looked down at the tiny shadow she cast on the sea-softened planks. It must be midday by now. They were too late. Blackbeard would have started murdering the prisoners. She tried to keep hope in her heart that the fisherman would have got to Blackbeard's fleet. They would have more time. Boubacar would still be alive. He had to be.

She looked around and realised Mr Marks had vanished. Meanwhile, Caesar was greeting some men on the dockside.

'Caesar! You rascal, I thought you were a dead man!' The man kissed him on the cheek and hollered out to a cooper who stopped dismantling his barrels and limped over.

'Blow me down! Black Caesar!' He cackled. 'You look thirsty!'

'Parched…' Caesar grinned. 'We were wrecked off the coast. I've no coin.'

'You can pay us with tales of your adventures!'

His friends were already drunk. They ignored Abigail and staggered off towards the town gates. A dog joined them. He was smaller than Governor Walker, but he greeted Caesar like an old friend.

'Caesar!' Abigail ran up to him and pulled on his sleeve. 'We need to find Mr Marks, get the Governor to secure the medicine and then get word to Blackbeard!'

'Mr Marks will go to the Governor for us. If we go with him we'll either be hanged or…' he paused for a moment. 'No, we will be hanged, simple as that.'

'Mr Marks is an idiot,' Gail said. 'What if they don't listen to him?'

'If they don't listen to a white free gentleman, what makes you think they will take a black man or grubby urchin seriously?'

Abigail touched her salt-knotted hair and looked down at her brown, bug-bitten arms. What with her bare feet and the cuts from the rocks on her legs, she realised couldn't have looked more feral if she tried.

'Go find yourself something to eat,' Caesar said. 'I need to come up with a plan.'

She followed them at a distance across a large square. There was a market where slave women were selling earthenware pots, red rice and cooked crabs. There was a lot of commotion as a child had been kicked by a mule and the cart owner was at odds with the child's master.

Abigail watched in disbelief as Caesar and his friends headed straight for a tavern.

Abigail slumped against a wall. Her fists balled. Her knuckle brushed against her pocket purse. She checked its contents. The coins she'd taken from the hostages and the small flask of powder. It had broken, presumably when the jolly boat had hit the rocks. Defeated, she walked back to the sellers in the square.

'Those be dog coins,' a man selling fruit laughed after she offered it. 'Pass it off on a slave. If you're brave enough to eat their muck.'

Abigail thought he was missing out if he thought slave food was muck. The food she'd had since leaving Sandy Hook was far more tasty than the bland beef stews and heavy dumplings her father had preferred. She inspected the coins. They might have less silver than a Spanish dollar bit, but surely they were worth a fruit or two. She was about to try her Yoruba out on a tired looking woman carrying a basketful of strange yellow bread when a bell at the docks sounded.

Abigail heard the faint chanting of the pirates before she saw the dark flag of *Queen Anne's Revenge* flying high over the tops of the dockside buildings. There was the boom of a cannon. A chimney broke off a dockside warehouse and cascaded down into the square. The noise was louder than thunder. People screamed. Mules bolted. More cannon fire. And then militiamen in red and blue came running from all directions.

Abigail made for a doorway and ducked as a second building was hit. Roof tiles tinkled like Christmas bells as they smashed into the flagstones. Caesar poked his head out of the tavern, a bottle of rum and a leg of turkey in his hands.

When he saw the devastation, he dropped the rum and the bottle rolled on the ground, spilling its contents. 'Gail! Gaaaaaiiiiil!'

She ran towards him. And he leant his arm on her shoulder. She took the turkey leg before he dropped that too.

'Blackbeard must think we're dead,' Caesar said. 'If he is laying siege to Charles Town that means he's already killed the hostages.'

'Even Boubacar?!' Abigail said.

More cannon fire sounded.

'When Thatch finds out we aren't dead and he murdered the hostages for nothing...' He looked out at the rubble in disbelief. 'The pox has turned him mad. He'll blame us for not getting word to him in time. He tried to kill me once already and I don't know any more good jokes to get us out of trouble. We need to hide.'

'Not until I know what happened to Boubacar,' Abigail said. 'The first rule of piracy is you don't abandon your family.'

'No, no, no. We don't abandon a living family! Dead families don't care,' Caesar said. 'If Thatch doesn't kill us on purpose, the way his mind is working, he'll get us killed by accident.'

'You aren't loyal to your captain either?' She spat.

'Listen Gail, the real first rule of piracy is to survive. You have to live to be a pirate!'

Musket fire. *Queen Anne's Revenge* was close enough to be in range of scrap shot.

'Let's hide and stay here. We can wait for him to leave, take the pardon and go on about our lives.'

Abigail looked at him, appalled.

'Thatch has lost his mind. He's been my best friend for years but I've never known him so reckless!'

'If he's killed Boubacar his temper will be nothing compared to mine!'

Abigail pushed past Caesar, taking a big bite of the turkey leg as she rounded the corner onto the dockside. *Queen Anne's Revenge* was broadside to the sea front. *Adventure* and *Revenge* were also positioned broadside to the sea wall and started firing their cannon. There was smashed wood and glass everywhere, broken bricks and twisted iron. Dozens of militiamen were busy preparing the cannons at the sea wall to fire. Abigail stomped towards the water, her feet picking up cuts on the way.

'Lad, get down!' A redcoat yelled at her.

'It's me they want to see,' she explained. 'They think you've hanged me and Caesar.'

'They are within musket range,' he warned. 'You'll get your little head blown off.'

'Not if they're aiming for it,' Abigail shouted back. 'They're drunk. I need to wave something. The King's colours! He hates that! Do you have a spare flag?'

She was passed one. 'You're mad, boy!'

She began walking up and down the sea wall, waving the cape-sized flag. Immediately a musket ball ripped a hole in it.

'Oi!' she shouted, 'use your eyes you mangy dogs!'

Another shot whizzed past her.

'Stupid pirates! They couldn't hit an elephant from…'

Abigail could hear the sea, a massive rushing in her ears. She couldn't see, she couldn't move… she had a pain in her head. Her legs ached. Images flashed before her eyes. Her bedroom at home, Mrs Phipps' pantry, the slaves in the sugar house…

She opened her eyes. She saw wood. There was a familiar smell. Immediately she knew where she was: *Queen Anne's Revenge*.

'Ah, you're awake,' the doctor said. 'Thatch wanted to cut you into chunks for shark bait. Fortunately for you, he was running a fever and passed out before the crew heard him.'

She sat up in bed. The sheets had been tucked in so she couldn't roll out. 'How long have I been asleep?'

'Nearly a week.' He smiled. 'But you've been awake before now. Do you not remember?'

She shook her head. Vague memories of vomiting in a chamber pot and drinking strong wine filtered into her mind. She looked over and saw Boubacar's shirt and breeches on a chair

– the clothes she'd been wearing for the last couple of months. She looked down and saw she was wearing a clean shirt and sailor's trousers.

The doctor looked amused. 'I did consider putting you in a dress, but I thought you might want to keep your identity a secret.'

'What happened to you?' Abigail said, pointing at his black eye.

'They caught me trying to escape again.'

'What happened to me?'

'From what I heard, a cannon exploded nearby, knocking you sideways. You cracked your head, the crew found you and now you're sound, and possibly safe. I'd like to see how you are on your feet. You were too woozy yesterday.'

'Did you find Caesar?'

The doctor shook his head. 'We didn't take much from Charles Town, just you and the medicine.'

'Blackbeard got his quicksilver?'

He grinned. 'I had the honour of giving it to him.'

'Oh, was it painful?'

'He screamed for his mother.'

They both laughed.

Abigail's glee was short lasting. The cool chill of what had happened washed into her like the fingers of a shallow wave creeping up the sand. She had failed to deliver the ransom note on time. Blackbeard had made good on his threats to execute the hostages and attack Charles Town. Boubacar must have died scared and alone. Was he hanged? Was he drowned? She couldn't bear thinking about it. And all this time she had been in bed. Not praying for him.

She had lost her last scrap of family. Her best friend. Her only friend. Images of him trapped and frightened kept creeping into her mind. He never knew that she'd tried to save him. She'd failed. Caesar had fled. She was alone. She was a pirate without a King's pardon. An outlaw. She had tarnished her soul, and her body was a mass of cuts and bruises. Her hair was sticky with salt and her hands and feet were leathery and common. She had no treasure, but even if she had, what would she do with it? Repair *Salt Pig*? For what? Go back to St Christopher's and free Nanny Inna? But how could she face her? Nanny Inna would never speak to her again now she'd lost Boubacar. Besides, she had no money. She had no future left.

'Where are you off to?' the doctor said, as she slipped out of the bed. 'You should stay put.'

Abigail didn't even hear him. She was limping a little as she staggered out of the compartment and onto the gun deck. The sunlight shone through the cannon hatches as she crept past the snoring pirates and up the wooden steps onto the main deck. Wind whipped her greasy hair. They were running close to the coast. There was a green smear of swamp in the distance. The smaller vessels in the fleet had gone ahead, carving their way between the boggy scraps of land. There were more boats now, presumably ones taken from Charles Town.

She leaned over the gunwale trying to see where they were heading, but all that lay ahead were flat, featureless sand bars.

She entered Blackbeard's cabin without knocking.

She found him slumped in his chair, looking worse than she'd ever seen him. On the table were his pistols. She immediately grabbed one, it was cold and heavy in her hands.

'I was cleaning them,' Blackbeard slurred. He sat up, plonked a half-open bottle of madeira on the table and swung his head round to look at her.

She hated him. Her life would be so different if he had never come to Sandy Point. He still didn't even realise what he had done. He'd taken her family from her, he'd turned her into a pirate. Everything was lost. She pointed the gun at his chest. She held her breath and pulled the trigger.

'It ain't loaded.' He gave a half smile.

Abigail threw it to the floor. 'You killed him!'

Blackbeard's large eyebrows rose. 'Who?'

'I'll kill you!'

He took a glug of wine. 'No offence lad, but I've got the King and every British colony on my tail. A squeaking pup like you ain't my most pressing concern.'

Abigail looked about the cabin for a weapon. She saw a small fruit knife and threw it at him. It missed and hit the wall. He didn't react.

'I hope they kill you!' Abigail said, tears in her eyes.

'I daresay that wish will be granted.' He looked at her and, shifting his weight in his chair, he drew his cutlass. He admired it glinting in the sunlight that came through the windows. 'But in that circumstance, you'll be strung up alongside me.'

Abigail stood shaking. She felt powerless. 'You'll never be hanged. You'll take the King's pardon.'

'I can't,' Blackbeard hiccoughed. 'I don't trust any governors. If I turn up at their ports with a fleet of ships, I won't get a chance to bargain for a pardon. Those weasels would sooner take me ships and claim the reward for my capture.'

'How big a fleet do you have now? You can't hide! You'll attract every British and Spanish warship to you.'

'It ain't just the law that endangers me. Our company is somewhat sober,' Blackbeard mumbled, his finger looking at the level in his wine bottle. 'A blasted confusion amongst us! Rogues are plotting and there is great talk of separation.'

'Wouldn't separation be good? It would be harder for the British to find a single ship than a fleet travelling together.'

'But then the men will want paying,' Blackbeard grumbled. 'I've got nothing to part with.'

'What about your secret treasure?' Abigail said. 'The one the Dutch assassins knew about. Charles Vane suspected you have it too.'

'Nobody but meself and the Devil knows where it be. And the longest liver should take all.'

'You must have some in reserve,' she reasoned. 'All the ships you've taken.'

'We only plundered a trifling amount from Charles Town. The men believe we're on our way to intercept a Spanish treasure fleet. When they find out there's no treasure fleet, they'll murder me faster than the British could hang me.'

'Well then, you've only one option.'

Blackbeard looked up at her. 'I do?'

'Scuttle your ship. Throw away all you've built. Your men will pity you, but they'll leave you alive. Then row yourself to the nearest governor as a penniless failed pirate.'

He looked at her, dumbfounded.

'You're very good at saving my life, Gail.' He stood up, swaying a little. 'As a reward, you may like to know, I didn't kill the hostages. I swapped them for the quicksilver. All except that friend of yours. I was considering selling him at the next port for rum.'

Abigail's heart pounded. 'Where is he?'

Blackbeard put his brace of pistols around his shoulders.

'Where is he?!' she yelled.

'I got him doing inventory. He's a good head on his shoulders.'

CHAPTER FIFTEEN

Blackbeard's Treasure

3rd June 1718

Blackbeard was shouting orders to Quartermaster Howard, telling him to signal to *Adventure* about a change of course. Abigail sped back down the steps to the gun deck, jumping over the cannon as the waking men blocked the gangway.

She dashed through the doors, past the carpenter's stores, down the hatch to the powder room, through the doors, down another ladder and into the hold.

It smelt bad down there. The bilge water sloshed over the stone ballast and the enormous beer barrels. The ship creaked and groaned, and rats pattered about. A rope swung like an empty gallows with the movement of the ship. A small amount of light came through the hatch of the gundeck above. It shone through the grate and cast a patch of chequered light on the wall that rocked back and forth with the ship.

'Boubacar?'

She couldn't see him and, for a brief moment, thought Blackbeard had lied to her.

'Gail?'

Her heart leapt.

'Where are you?'

'I'm by the main mast.'

She jumped onto the nearest barrel, avoiding the stinking bilge water and climbed up onto the next barrel, making her way towards the mast that passed through the hold and into the keel at the very centre of the ship. Sure enough, there, sitting on a barrel above the bilge water clutching charcoal and paper, was Boubacar. She let out an excited squeak as they embraced.

'I thought you weren't going to wake up!' he said wrapping his arms around her.

'I'm sorry I couldn't get to Charles Town on time,' she sobbed. 'We were wrecked on the rocks. Then when we got to town, Caesar ran away. I got blown up by a cannon.'

'I know, I know…'

Suddenly, there was an enormous sound. A booming, snapping, warping of wood. The ship was screaming. The children were thrown apart as the barrels they were standing on shifted beneath them. Like a flash, Boubacar grabbed a rope that was tied around the main mast.

'Hold onto me.'

The light shaft flashed as the entire boat tilted. Abigail narrowly avoided trapping her foot between the moving barrels as she reached out to grasp Boubacar's shoulders. The barrels slipped sideways, moving as easily as if they were empty. Boubacar placed his feet onto the mast and Abigail copied, just as the barrel rolled out from under them. The whole ship was tilting further and further.

There were more terrifying splitting sounds and water began gushing through the bow.

'We've got to get out!' Abigail said in a panic. 'I didn't think he would actually do it. Blackbeard's scuttled his ship!'

'She's not steady yet!' Boubacar shouted as more barrels shifted position, slamming into each other and causing a further cascade.

'We don't have long!' Abigail made to step on a nearby barrel but Boubacar stopped her.

The barrel rolled away. Then the ballast rocks at the bottom of the ship began cascading downwards, blocking the hatch Abigail had come through. The children could hear the gun carriages on the deck above rolling and crashing into each other. The ship tilted further.

They sat on the steeply angled mast like it was a horse. The deck above was now in front of them, the water rising all around. The wooden beams popped and splintered over the roar of seawater as it poured in around them.

Abigail looked either side of the mast. 'I think I can make it back to the hatch,' she said. 'It's underwater, but if we dive down, we can get through.'

'She's not settled yet,' Boubacar shouted. 'The ballast will crush you. She's not done listing. Stay put.'

There was a great movement and the entire ship dropped a couple of feet. A horrible feeling seized Abigail. She would never leave this place. The thought made something in her throat close up. She couldn't breathe. She wasn't even in the water and she couldn't breathe.

Boubacar reached forward and grasped her arm. He began a song of Nanny Inna's.

'Allah, accu lawol fulbe,' they sang.

Abigail shrieked when the water reached her feet.

'See the hatch to the gundeck?' Boubacar shouted. Abigail saw that the grate had partially fallen away and a gap had appeared at the top. It looked large enough to squeeze through. 'When the water is high enough, we can get through it, but we have to wait until it has risen.'

A chill ran down Abigail's spine. When the water was that high, they wouldn't have long to leave the ship before the way out was underwater.

'Now!' Boubacar shouted.

Abigail dropped into the water. The current moved against her, flowing away from the hatch. The memory of Caesar's angry voice echoed in her mind. She held her breath and kicked her legs as hard as she could. To her astonishment, she got to the grate before Boubacar. The water wasn't high enough for her to pull herself out but she could reach up and put her fingers on the side of the hatch so that the current didn't pull her away.

Boubacar appeared next to her, coughing into the falling water. It was pouring down through the half-fallen grate and onto their heads, making it hard to catch a breath. As the water level rose, Abigail found she could get a better grip. It was enough to pull her chest up over the water streaming through the grate so she could see how much room they had to squeeze through. To her dismay, although there was a gap at the top of the hatch left by the dislodged grate, it was far narrower than she had first thought. Boubacar tried pushing the grate to displace it further but he wasn't strong enough. He held onto the surround, pushed himself up out of the waterfall of seawater and kicked the loose grate with both feet. It fell back, clearing the hatch of any obstacles. The waterflow around them doubled in intensity. Abigail struggled to maintain her grip. Boubacar's reached out to her. She grabbed his arm and kicked with all her might.

Both children were standing knee deep on the side of the hatch looking out into the gundeck. It was like a fantastic dream with the whole ship tilted sideways. Above them, sunlight streamed through the cannon hatches. Below was a mess of hammocks, cannon, boxes and cannon balls submerged on what used to be the port side of the ship.

'We're not moving,' Abigail panted as the water stopped flowing. The sea level on both sides of the hatch was now even. Waves lapped softly up her legs, but instead of the usual sway, the ship itself was still. 'Why aren't we moving with the sea?'

'We must have run aground.' Boubacar clung to the hatch and pointed at the broken cannon rope above them. 'Let's climb up out of the gunport.'

Abigail nodded, and watched him climb on the edge of the hatch. He made a leap for a frayed rope that used to hold a cannon in place. He grabbed it with one arm and Abigail took his position on the hatch. She couldn't reach the rope herself so he held out his arm. Once she had a grip of the rope, they gingerly climbed up the steeply sloping deck towards the square of daylight. Abigail followed him out, using her last bit of strength to brace herself against the sides of the small hatch. Fresh air whipped Abigail's hair and she felt a sense of euphoria the moment the sun kissed her face.

They sat panting on the side of the ship's hull. The air was pungent with exposed seaweed. *Queen Anne's Revenge* was embedded on a sandbank. The lighter sand was visible only a few yards under the surface before it sloped down into deeper, darker water. Many of the pirates had swum further away from the wreck and some, in the distance, were heading for another sandbar, where, much to Abigail's surprise, *Adventure* had also run aground.

'We need to follow them.' Boubacar pointed over the water. 'They're already starting to board *Revenge*. They'll leave without us.'

Abigail busied herself by climbing up the side of the ship towards the gunwale. The wood had already started to dry, and she looked back to see her wet footprints like a shadow, marking her progress up the boat. It seemed larger on its side and dreamlike to be standing at this angle.

'Are you listening?' Boubacar said, looking for a way down.

She reached where the deck met the side of the ship, and called back to Boubacar, 'Do you remember what Bill called the devil?'

Boubacar was exasperated. 'You never listen.'

'It was a seam, wasn't it? Which one was it?'

'The longest one that goes round the ship.'

'This one?' she said, pointing at a messy line covered in pitch.

'I suppose.'

'Do you have a knife?'

'It's blunt,' he said, handing it to her.

'Uh huh,' she grunted, and started peeling back the pitch with the knife blade.

'You're getting it filthy!'

'Blackbeard told me,' Abigail said, picking off small bits of black with her fingernails, 'that no one knows where his treasure is hidden except him and the Devil.'

'If it even exists,' Boubacar snorted.

'Remember what Bill said about why Blackbeard's crew liked him so much?' she asked. 'Because he did the most unpopular jobs on his ships. Like…'

Boubacar finished her sentence, '… paying the devil.'

Boubacar looked down and saw what she was holding in her hands. Something in the thick curl of tar was sparkling.

'Are those diamonds?'

'And more gemstones!' She laughed, prizing out the small stones from their sticky black host. 'He buried his treasure in the ship itself!'

'Just a handful of these is worth a fortune!' Boubacar gasped in amazement.

'We can go back to St Christopher's! We can buy your family and set them free,' she squealed.

Boubacar beamed.

'Our family,' he said.

***

The sun had begun to drop in the sky. The pirates were long gone, sailing away on *Revenge*. They had left *Queen Anne's Revenge* and *Adventure* stranded on the sandbar. Boubacar and Abigail had spent hours picking away at the devil, unearthing tiny precious jewels which they carefully placed into Abigail's pocket purse. They were so absorbed in the task that Abigail forgot to complain about her thirst.

The light dimmed. The wind frothed the sea, wailing as it sped through the tangled rigging. Spray splattered them. As the sky grew darker,

Boubacar noticed some fires far in the distance, towards the inlet.

'It could be a hamlet,' he said. 'Or a native village.'

Abigail shivered, gripping her bare feet with her hands to try and warm them. Her stomach growled but she knew they couldn't leave the wreck until the water was calmer. A squall threatened them. She half hoped it would rain so she could catch the water in her mouth. Clouds blocked out any light from the stars. Boubacar wrapped his arm around Abigail and they cuddled together for warmth.

Abigail saw it first and shook Boubacar awake. The night was calmer and stars appeared between the gaps in the cloud.

There was a light out at sea. Boubacar stood up. He could barely make out what it was in the dark,

'It's a lugger.'

'We don't have anything to signal to it,' Abigail said dismayed.

'It is coming this way.'

'Maybe it wants to salvage what it can from the wrecks.'

'At night? What if it is the militia?' Boubacar said, pulling her down. 'We've got no weapons.'

They watched silently as the small boat approached. Abigail thought about the reward for capturing a pirate. She was worth £30 to anyone alive. That was nearly two years of an average sailor's wage. She flattened herself on the wood, trying not to move lest she be seen. The boat moved closer. She could see it silhouetted against the dark grey water. There were three men aboard. She could hear their voices carry over the waves. They were speaking in Igbo.

'Any second now they are going to see us!' she murmured to Boubacar.

'We'll call for help. Not a word about the treasure,' he whispered. Then he shouted, 'A chọrọ m enyemaka!'

Abigail joined in. 'Biko!'

There was laughter from the boat.

'Ahoy! Are you stuck?'

Abigail couldn't believe it. She recognised the voice at once.

'The first rule of being a pirate,' shouted the man from the lugger, 'is don't get stranded on a wreck.'

'Caesar!' Boubacar screamed in excitement. 'Captain! We're up here!'

Getting onto the lugger in choppy waters was no small endeavour. It took three attempts for Caesar to throw the rope. Boubacar tied it off, but the boat moved about as they tried to descend the slippery side of *Queen Anne's Revenge*. The lugger was in danger of smashing itself against the hull of the bigger ship as it bobbed like a bucking mule in the wash. Abigail sliced her foot on a barnacle before climbing onto the rope and inching to the boat, upside down like a velvet monkey on a vine. She was close to the mast of the lugger when her grip failed her. She fell into the blackness, sideways into the sea.

A familiar arm caught her.

By the lamplight she saw the friendly faces of Uzzy and Koby, and then the happy grin of

Caesar. Boubacar had managed the descent far faster than she had, and both he and Abigail hugged Caesar so tightly that the big man chuckled.

They made for the land, aiming for the rocks where they found fresh water and set up a fire. Abigail, her cut foot raised on a hogshead barrel, devoured the roasted yams and a pitcher of the tea that the crew made. The clouds cleared completely and the stars above twinkled like gemstones in pitch as Koby and Uzzy, with a little translation from Caesar, described their adventure of stealing the lugger and rescuing Caesar from being arrested.

Later, as everyone else slept, Abigail turned to Caesar and whispered, 'I thought you were going to stay in Charles Town?'

'I'm going back to my captain,' he said. 'I'll see you and the boy to safety first.'

'You pick strange friends.'

'And you pick strange enemies. You fixated on Thatch who, despite what you say, only wreaks damage to property. He likes to make drama, to make himself seem scary. But he only hurts people who try to kill him first.'

'Governor Walker!'

Caesar chuckled. 'He knew I'd rescue him. He has to seem bloodthirsty to keep his crew in line. Like he wouldn't have let that boy on the *Crowley* die. Ships wouldn't stop for him if they didn't fear his name. He isn't as evil as he wants you to believe.'

'He scuttled the ship while I was down in the hold!'

'You got out. I admit he doesn't think too much about the consequences but he's hardly as cruel as someone like your old man.'

Abigail slowly nodded. 'That's probably true. Charles Vane said my father did all sorts of nasty things on his ship during the war.'

Caesar prodded her in the arm. 'That's what is strange about you. A normal person would have sought revenge on Vane. He killed your father. Why did you care about Thatch?'

'I suppose it wasn't really about my father.' Abigail exhaled. 'After Blackbeard attacked,

Boubacar's brother was sold. Boubacar stopped talking to me.'

'So you were seeking revenge for Boubacar and not your father?'

'I don't think I like my father anymore,' Abigail said softly. 'Boubacar is my family.'

'Thatch is mine.'

'When we were in Charles Town you said he was going to get you killed. What happened to the real first rule of piracy?'

'Ah, you mean the first rule of piracy is to survive?' He clicked his tongue. 'The only point of surviving is to have friends to live for.'

Abigail was too tired to respond. Her eyes slowly closed as her head fell back into the sand.

The Boſton News-Letter

PUBLISHED BY AUTHORITY

From Monday October 17 to Monday October 24, 1720

An express arrived at Charles Town from Port Royall, which advises that Capt. Rackham, alias Calico Jack, is out on the Pirating account again. On Sept. 5th, His Excellency Woodes Rodgers, Governour of New Providence &c. issued a Proclamation that Capt. Rackham and his company are Pirates and enemies of the Crown of Great Britain, and are to be treated and deemed by all His Majeſty's subjects as Felons. This proclamation has done nothing to diminish Rackham's fervency. Capt. Rackham, associate of notorious Pirate Capt. Vane, commands a sloop call'd *William*, owned by and belonging to Capt. John Ham and stolen therefrom on the 22nd August last. Rackham's company notoriously includes two Women, by name Anne Bonny & Mary Read.

Most recently, said sloop attacked fishing vessels and merchant ships around the Island of Cuba. The only merchant vessel surviving according to an account by Master. B. Buckler was a thirty-tonne sloop of the newly formed Buckler & Buckler Co. of which he is owner. Capt. Gail Buckler of the said sloop *Salt Pig* left an account which credited their survival on the Kindness of the Women crewe and requested their mercy should be taken into account in the event of their capture.

Meanwhile the South Sea company reported they lost two sloops laden with wine, and a sloop from Jamaica bound for Philadelphia with a cargo of slaves and tobacco was also attacked. The likely culprit is the Pirate Capt. Vane who pilots a six-gun sloop called *Lark*. He still remains at large, a scourge of the seas…

Abigail's Dictionary

Addlepate 18th-century insult. Addle means rotten or spoiled and pate is an old-fashioned word for head, so this literally means rotten head.

Admiral of the Black person who commands a fleet of pirate ships. A way of referring to the pirate with the most authority.

Bamboozle to deceive other ships as to your ship's origin or nationality by flying a flag other than your own. This was a common practice of pirates.

Black flag flag signalling that a pirate ship was about to attack. Scary, but not as bad as a red flag which signalled that no quarter was to be given, meaning the pirates wanted to kill everyone on board.

Blunderbuss type of gun with a large barrel that doesn't require aiming. Also, an insult referring to someone who is clumsy or unsubtle.

Boatswain (or **Bosun**) person in charge of the upkeep of a ship and the most senior person in the crew.

Jolly boat a small vessel used to transport goods and people from ships to shore (and back again).

Carib indigenous people of the Caribbean (actually the name for a group of people from South America). The indigenous population of the Caribbean also included the Taíno and Lucayan people.

Charles Town modern day Charleston, South Carolina.

Clew to raise (or lower) a square sail by ropes called the clew lines.

Flux illness which we now call amoebic dysentery which was known in the 18th century as 'the bloody flux', and was a common, lethal disease aboard ships. It was a fever with stomach cramps, vomiting and diarrhoea which could spread quickly and kill everyone on board.

Forecastle upper deck of a ship forward of the foremast.

Gaff rig In the early 18th century, Bermuda sloops like the fictional *Salt Pig* were gaff rigged. This meant the sail had a beam at the top (a gaff) and the bottom (a boom). The sail was square instead of triangular so it could catch more wind and go faster.

Gundiguts 18th-century insult meaning a rude, unpleasant person with a big stomach.

Gun worm twisty screw (a bit like a modern corkscrew) used for cleaning out gun barrels. Any debris left in the gun after it was shot could cause it to explode.

Gunwale the wooden barrier around the top deck of a ship. It often had hatches for cannon.

Jacobite someone who felt George I wasn't the rightful king of Great Britain and that James Stuart should be king instead. There were a lot of Jacobites in the British Caribbean at the time this story is set.

Keel hauling punishment where the victim was tied to a rope and dragged under the bottom of a ship and back onto the deck. Although it wasn't always a death sentence, many died from drowning or hitting their heads on the bottom of the vessel. The barnacles which lived on the bottom of ships could also case serious cuts which would become infected.

King's colours British flag later called the Union Jack. Ships working for the King would fly the King's colours to signal to other ships who they were.

Letter of marque licence that authorised a private person to attack vessels at war with the issuer. This enabled people to effectively become legal pirates and they were often used in the wars between European countries in the time this story is set.

Long-seed patwa word for 'old'. Patwa is spoken primarily in Jamaica and comes from a mixture of English with West African languages. Back in the 18th century it was in the process of being created.

Lubber (landlubber) a person unfamiliar with sailing.

Lugger boat that uses lug sail(s) which are four sided.

Maroon escaped slave of the West Indies in the 17th and 18th centuries. Their descendants were also called 'maroons'. They mixed with the indigenous people on the islands and formed their own communities and culture. They often had to fight to defend themselves against the white colonists.

Powder monkey boy who took the gunpowder charge from where it was prepared to the gundeck of a ship. You couldn't prepare the charge near the cannons as one spark would cause it to detonate.

Privateer private person who engages in sea warfare legally (not as part of a navy). A king or queen issued letters of marque which protected privateers from accusations of piracy but allowed them to attack (and pillage) enemy ships, including rogue pirate ships.

Puff guts 18th-century insult meaning a person with a big stomach.

Quartermaster senior member of a ship's crew, usually in charge of navigation, managing the crew's duties and dealing out punishments.

Shabbaroon 18th-century insult meaning a scruffy, mean person.

Shipworm type of barnacle that ate through the wooden hulls of ships. If a ship couldn't get into dock and scrape them off, it risked sinking.

Shroud part of the rigging that keeps the mast in place on a ship. Pirates and sailors also used them as rope ladders to climb up the masts.

Slave market depending on the location, a slave market was either a place where people were bought and sold as slaves or it was where people who were enslaved traded with each other. They would make items that they could sell so they could buy things to make their lives a little better. The danger was that as they weren't recognised as people in the eyes of the law if anyone stole from them, they had no way to seek justice.

Sloop large sailing boat with a single mast. Pirates preferred them as they were nimble in the water and had shallow bottoms which made them harder to run aground.

Snapsack canvas shoulder bag with a simple drawstring.

St Christopher's Island modern day St Kitts.

Treasure anything of value. For the pirates in this story this would have included gold dust, gemstones, people they could sell as slaves, tobacco, sugar and wine.

Yard wooden beam that the sail hangs from. The yardarm is the very end of the beam.

The Crew

Henry Avery or **Every** (1659–????) English. Tricked by the Spanish into servitude which forced him to fight his way free. He plundered vessels and set up a pirate kingdom on Madagascar. He escaped capture, most notoriously by bribing the governor of Nassau. No one is sure what happened to him but his story inspired thousands.

Sam Bellamy aka **Black Sam** (1689–1717) English. Sailor who turned pirate because he needed money to impress his girlfriend's parents. With the help of Paulsgrave Williams he captured a huge ship, the *Whydah*. He is famous for a speech he gave trying to persuade a captured merchant crew of the virtue of the freedom of pirate life. He died when the *Whydah* sank in a storm.

Stede Bonnet (1688–1718) Barbadian. Plantation owner turned pirate. He had a family back on Barbados but abandoned them, presumably because he was enchanted by stories of pirates at sea. After Blackbeard scuttled his ship, Stede took the pardon but turned pirate again later. He wasn't a skilled sailor and was caught soon after and hanged.

Anne Bonny (1697–1721) Irish. Born to a mother and father who weren't married, her father disguised her as a boy and took her to America. She married James Bonny when she was still a teenager and later had a relationship with Calico Jack. She fought alongside Jack and Mary Read, another cross-dressing female pirate. When they were captured, she and Mary claimed they were pregnant to avoid execution. It is likely Anne died in prison but there is no record of her execution or what became of her child.

Black Caesar (????–1718) African (unknown which country). Little is written about Black Caesar (there are a number of pirates who went by that name). All we do know is he was likely a slave who escaped, and was a brilliant, loyal member of Blackbeard's crew. So much so that in Blackbeard's final battle Caesar was caught trying to blow up his sloop rather than let the British take him.

Benjamin Hornigold (1680–1719) English. A crafty pirate captain who commanded Nassau. He refused to attack British ships and took the King's pardon. Afterwards he worked for Woodes Rogers hunting Charles Vane but died at sea when his ship was caught in a hurricane.

Henry Jennings (????–????) British Bermudan. Wealthy privateer. He turned pirate when he illegally attacked a Spanish salvage camp. He had a rivalry with Hornigold and Black Sam. He was Charles Vane's captain until he took the pardon. He retired to Bermuda.

Olivier Lavasseur aka **La Buse** (1690–1730) French. Pirate who famously left clues to his hidden treasure. It is said to be worth over a billion US dollars and no one, to this day, has discovered it.

Mr Marks (????–????) British colonist in North America. From Charles Town (now Charleston, South Carolina). Really did accompany two of Blackbeard's pirates to negotiate the release of hostages aboard the captured *Crowley* for exchange of medicines. After capsizing the boat, Marks and the pirates tried to make it to town on a raft and were rescued by fishermen. Blackbeard threatened the town anyway.

Jack Rackham aka **Calico Jack** (1682–1720) English. Quartermaster to Charles Vane. He later led a mutiny against him, taking control of *Lark*. He was romantically involved with Anne Bonny and together they plundered many ships until they were eventually captured by the British. He was hanged in Port Royal.

Woodes Rogers (1679–1732) English. Famous sailor, privateer and slave trader. After circumnavigating (sailing all the way around) the world he was sued by his crew for their fair share of the expedition profits. Rogers became bankrupt. He had been badly injured on the voyage with a musket shot lodged in his face. He later sailed to Madagascar and successfully convinced the pirates there to petition Queen Anne for mercy. He then was chosen to rid the Caribbean of pirates. In 1718 he became the first Royal Governor of the Bahamas but had little to no financial support from Britain. Although he executed many pirates, a combination of a war breaking out with Spain and his own ill health forced him back to England. There he was put in debtors' prison. After he helped write the popular book *A General History of the Robberies and Murders of the Most Notorious Pyrates* in 1724, he was once again a hero and returned to the Bahamas as governor. He never recovered from his ill health, however, and died in 1732.

Edward Thatch or **Teach**, aka **Blackbeard** (1680–1718) English (probably from Bristol). Joined Benjamin Hornigold's crew and was put in charge of his own sloop. In 1717 he took a large slave ship called *La Concorde* without a fight as its crew and cargo were sick and unable to defend themselves. He renamed it *Queen Anne's Revenge*, hinting to his Jacobite sympathies. He was a showman, setting fuses in his beard alight when attacking merchant ships. After *Queen Anne's Revenge* ran aground, he tricked his crew by selling them to North Carolina's governor, Charles Eden, and taking the pardon for himself. However, he soon returned to pirating. He was bribing Eden to protect him but he wasn't paying the governor of Virginia who ordered his men to hunt him down. Blackbeard fought to the death with Robert Maynard on November 21st 1718 at Ocracoke Island. After killing him, Maynard hung Blackbeard's severed head from his bowsprit as a warning to all pirates.

Charles Vane (1680–1721) English. From Wapping in London, a poor area where public executions were held. As a boy, he may have witnessed pirates being executed. This didn't put him off becoming one of the most ruthless, violent pirates of all time. He worked under Henry Jennings but, unlike his old pirate captain, he didn't mind attacking British merchant ships and torturing those aboard. After fleeing a fight, his men voted against him and forced him out of his own ship. He was eventually caught after being rescued from an uninhabited island and was executed in 1721.

Paulsgrave Williams (????–????) British colonist in North America. From Rhode Island. A jeweller who turned pirate after meeting Sam Bellamy. They worked successfully together until the sinking of the *Whydah* when Black Sam was drowned. After taking the pardon in September 1718, Williams was soon back at sea, serving as quartermaster under his old accomplice Olivier Levasseur off the coast of Africa. Rumours are that sailors still called him 'Captain' to get on his good side. By 1723 he had retired from piracy.

William Wragg (1714–????) British colonist in North America. From Charles Town (now Charleston, South Carolina). Son of Samual Wragg, who was a member of Carolina colony's governing council. Taken hostage when *Crowley* was attacked in the siege of Charles Town.